# MARRIED TO THE MOUNTAIN MAN

## COURAGE COUNTY CURVES

MIA BRODY

1

# BRENNON

I DRUM MY FINGERS ALONG THE STEERING WHEEL, staring up at the imposing columns of the cathedral. My brother's wedding is today, and I'm expected to be here. I'd rather be at home where I don't have to deal with the whispers and the pitying stares from my family's high society friends.

They were my friends too. But the stroke stole the ability to communicate from me. I can mutter a few words here and there. Nothing comes out right. It all gets stuck inside my head and despite the best speech therapy that money can buy and numerous consults with neurosurgeons, no one can put my brain back together again.

No one can turn back the clock and change the

fact that at thirty, I had a massive stroke. They called it a patent foramen ovale, which means I had a fuckin' hole in my heart. It went undetected for years until the day it caused the stroke.

Overnight, I changed from a billionaire CEO to a rambling guy who pissed himself and had to relearn how to walk. I did it. I regained everything but my ability to speak. It's still not enough.

I'm not the same man I was, so I retreated. I built my own cabin in the mountains of Courage County, far from the family business.

I should have just sent a wedding gift and called it done. But I was curious about the woman my brother would marry. She has to be a gold digger, a fair-weather woman who will be gone the moment my brother needs support or companionship.

Forcing myself from the car, I nod at the men in suits that are carefully guarding the fancy cathedral here in Asheville. I don't even bother trying to speak, not when it's clear they know who I am. I am an Abernathy and here that inspires admiration and respect. But mostly, well-earned fear.

I move through the winding halls without an escort or a guide, not eager for this reunion. I wonder if it's too late to send the gift and duck out.

By now, the first look should be starting. Mom will want everyone gathered in one room so there can be dozens of family photos. After all, an event's success is directly proportional to how much envy it causes in one's upper crust friends.

I slip into the room. Cool air, ornate marble surfaces, and gold filigree scream that this is not the place where the poor worship. No, this is for sell-outs like us who make our money lying, cheating, and stealing from everyone around us. But at least, we look good doing it.

My eyes instantly go to Cadence, the name I recognize from the wedding invitation. She's a goddess with long, black flowing hair that's coiffed up in a careful bun with a few tendrils framing her heart-shaped face. Her bright, blue eyes are filled not with anticipation at the events of the coming day but anxiety. Her plump red lips are so damn kissable. And those curves make my mouth water and leave me aching to hold her close.

There's just one problem. She's my brother's girl. She's wearing a wedding dress. She's marrying that lucky bastard today. She carefully adjusts her veil and when she catches my eye in the mirror, she turns.

I lick my suddenly dry lips. I want to tell her to run away with me instead. I want to yell at her that she's making the worst mistake of her life. That my brother—God forgive me—is a heartless bastard who will do nothing more than crush her hopes and dreams.

But there's nothing to say. The words might come out as gibberish anyway.

Cadence gives me a guarded smile. She steps forward, her voice quiet and lilting. She's a melody I forgot but the moment I hear it, I know every note by heart. "Hi, I'm Cadence."

I nod to her. Maybe it's a good thing that I can barely speak. Because if I could, only the filthiest words would be coming out of my mouth. Things that would make this curvy goddess blush for days.

"It's nice to meet the last member of the family," she says. Her knuckles are white from where she's clutching the folds of the wedding gown. It looks like some monstrosity my mom forced her to wear. It wouldn't surprise me if those are real diamonds sewed into the bodice.

I nod again, rather than try to speak.

"Your family is very nice." She stumbles over the word and we both know why. They're vipers, every last one of them. Up until my stroke, I was the cruelest of them. But having your entire family turn on you when you're alone in the hospital changes you.

Since I won't risk saying anything, I put my hand on her shoulder. Even with the thin white material that signifies she belongs to my brother, the touch still feels right. It feels like I should be doing this every day, comforting her and protecting her.

She closes her eyes briefly, steadying herself.

But before she can say anything, my brother and his friends are stumbling into the room. I drop my hand and turn to them. I should smile or something. I think I read once that families are happy to see each other. But whoever wrote that book never had a family like mine.

Andrew already reeks of alcohol. He always does these days. I used to joke that it wasn't a holiday until Dad had bought Andrew out of a DUI and made his latest arrest go away. Back then, I thought that shit was funny. Now, it's disgusting.

"Oh, good. You met her," Andrew slurs. He sways on his feet.

I glance at Cadence, and her entire expression has gone blank. She turns to the mirror and pretends to fuss with her dress and hair, ignoring her husband-to-be. I'm guessing this isn't the magical first look that most couples have on their wedding day. Figures Andrew would be marrying as part of a business merger. I should have seen that coming.

I reach for his tie and quickly undo the sloppy knot. Cadence is sweet. She doesn't fit in here among them. There's no calculating gleam in her eye, no streak of cruelty that she's waiting to unleash.

"She's a fuckin' hippo," he complains as if she's not in the room.

He makes a wheezing sound when I tighten the tie harder than necessary around his throat. He'll never appreciate those big tits or those ample hips. He'll never watch with awe and wonder as she climbs into his lap. He'll never look at her and see his queen.

I glance toward Cadence, but there's not even a hint of surprise on her face. Fuckin' jack ass. This isn't the first time he's talked about her like this and certainly not the first time he's done it in front of her. No, the only thing in her expression is steely determination. She must need him badly if she's willing to put up with my brother.

"Put her fat ass on a diet," one of the groomsmen suggests. He's dealing cards to the other groomsmen.

I glare in the direction of the five guys I used to hang out with when I was together with my brother. Were they always like this? How did I never notice?

"Everyone knows that whales don't diet," another groomsmen quips and all of them break into cruel laughter that has my blood boiling.

I finish his tie and drop my hands, squeezing them into fists. She wants him. She's chosen him. She knows what she's getting.

"Hey, Cadence," my brother leers. I hate the sound of her name on his lips. I hate the way he's looking at her and the things he must think about her. His lips twist in a smile that's anything but kind. "Can whales even orgasm?"

That's how my older brother ends up on the floor with a bloody nose, crying like the little bitch he is. It takes two of his asshole friends to pull me off of him because I might barely be able to speak but I'm still in fighting shape. Hell, I'm in better shape now than I ever was.

Somewhere in my brain, Cadence's gasp registers. But I don't even look at her. I'm too damn intent on putting my brother in his place.

"What the hell is your problem?" Andrew demands as he scrambles to his feet, holding his nose. "Is your brain still scrambled, you dumb mute?"

Maybe the barb would have stung once upon a time, but I have a bigger mission in life now. It's to protect and love my girl. Yeah, Cadence is mine and as soon as the realization blooms in my chest, I know it's the truth. Summoning all of my focus, I manage to growl a single word at him, "Mine."

He makes a sound that might be a chuckle. It's hard to tell around all the blood that's leaking onto his tuxedo and the way he's cradling his nose. "Wait. You want lardo?"

I nod at him. Growing up, he'd never give me what I wanted. We were always in fierce competition and even though he was older than me, I was still the favored son. He might not want to give me her, but it doesn't matter. Because I will keep fighting him until he surrenders her.

"Oh, this is too good. The whale and the idiot." His voice has taken on a nasally quality and he has to stop to shove tissue up his nostrils.

Under his eyes are already turning purple. He'll have the best surgeon in town reset the damn thing within an hour. The only thing I truly hurt was his pride. "Tell you what, little bro. You can have her. But you handle mom and dad."

My parents may not admit it but they'll both be relieved to marry Cadence off to me. They'll still get what they want while being able to use Andrew in another of their schemes. They'll probably marry him off to a rich heiress that he can make miserable for a few years before she gets the good sense to divorce him.

"Jeremy, call my surgeon then get me a clean shirt," he demands of his assistant. The man is supposed to be his friend, but you wouldn't know that by the way Andrew talks to him.

He turns toward the side door, the one that will let him escape like the rat he is. "You and tubby have fun making little piglets."

I growl and step toward him. All it takes is that one move and he's scurrying away. Sounds like he's laughing under his breath. But I don't care. I just laid claim to my bride. Now all I have to do is convince her to walk down the aisle with me instead.

My knuckles throb, already bruising. There are ways to throw a punch and protect the knuckles, but I didn't do that. I wanted the punches that would inflict the most pain possible on my brother. Even now I want to run after him. I want to demolish him until he's nothing more than a stain on the asphalt next to the dumpster outside.

I turn to Cadence, content now that I know she's safe from my brother's barbs. It doesn't matter whether it's physical or verbal, I'll always be the man who defends her. It takes a superhuman level of concentration to ground out the words, "Marry. Me."

## 2
## CADENCE

"How are you doing?" I grip my phone tighter as I ask the question and fight the nerves rolling in my stomach. Never did I imagine that I would be having a phone conversation with my father while he's in jail, awaiting trial. They deemed him a flight risk and set a bond of millions despite the fact that he's never left the country and has no prior convictions for any crime.

"Your old man is doing just fine, sweet pea," he reassures me in that gravelly smoker's voice. "Now you tell me what you're doing today."

For a moment, my heart beats faster as I worry that he knows. Today, I'm marrying his arch nemesis. Or at least, the son of his arch nemesis. Andrew is no prize. He's cruel and manipulative, just like his father.

But Andrew's father cooked the books. He made it out like my father has swindled his investors. Phony evidence that he submitted to a crooked judge, all in a desperate bid to get his hands on my father's technology.

So, I did the only thing I could do. I went to Jackson Abernathy and pleaded for mercy. I begged, a fact that would shame my father if he knew. But he doesn't know. He'll never know. If I'm careful, I can keep him in the dark about this sham of a marriage.

"I'm working on a big marketing project then going out with the girls for sushi," I answer. I'm the marketing director for his company. Our company. My name is on it, same as his. Only with one key difference. I hold a sixty-one percent share in it.

He started the company with my mom when she was alive. She was his queen, and he would have laid the world at her feet. That's why he gave her a sixty-one percent share. But she passed just a few years after that, and her shares became mine according to the will. Not that it mattered.

My mom wasn't alive to see what the company would become. My dad was still a poor inventor, a tinkerer when she passed. His success wouldn't come until nearly two decades later when he would discover a way to revolutionize the battery industry. With his technology, the Abernathy family will be able to manufacture electric cars that run three times as long and only require a charging time of less than ten minutes. It's unheard of and it'll give them the edge to own the industry within a matter of years, maybe even months.

"I'll be out of here real soon, and things can go back to normal," Dad says. He's making promises he won't be able to keep. I've already consulted a lawyer, some second-rate attorney that didn't have the sense to be afraid of the Abernathy name. But even Mr. Flunked-the-Bar-Six-Times could see the writing on the wall. The case against my father is airtight.

For a second, my mind drifts back in time.

"See, four plus four is eight. It's always going to be eight," Daddy says as he spears the eighth dinosaur-shaped noodle on a fork. The glow of the streetlight illuminates the can of cold pasta, a staple of my childhood.

I write the number on my homework sheet, sighing my relief. The last math problem is finally solved.

He offers me the eighth dinosaur, and I take it

from the fork before peering into the empty can. "Where are your eight, daddy?"

He rubs his belly. It used to be round and jiggled when he laughed. It's flat there now and he never laughs. At least, not like he did when mom was here. "Daddy ate a big lunch. He's still full. Now come, sleepy time."

I reach for the lever on the passenger seat and ease it back, just enough that it doesn't crush our belongings in the backseat. Daddy covers me with a blanket that smells stinky, humming a song under his breath.

"Will we go back home soon?" I ask, my little mind still puzzling over the fact that we left. Daddy said we were going car camping, but it's been a lot of days and we don't have beds anymore.

"Soon," he says, and his eyes get that sad look in them. They've had that sad look since mommy went to heaven. I think that's why we had to go car camping. "You have to tell me something, Cadence."

He sounds serious so I pop open an eyeball to look at him. I hope he doesn't make me say I like math. Numbers are boring and hard. "OK."

"Sometimes, life is scary and sad," he says. "But everything can change in a minute, and I need you to tell me you won't ever, ever give up. Promise me."

This sounds like a serious promise, so I hold out my pinky finger, just like I do with my friends at recess. "Promise."

He wraps his big work-roughened finger around mine and gives me a soft smile. "That's my girl."

Dad's voice brings me back to the present as he instructs, "You eat all the sushi you want. You charge it to my account."

He's a millionaire now. Well, he was. His assets have all been seized but he doesn't know that either. It's another thing I've kept from him. After years of growing up so poor, he loves the chance to spoil me. I can't bear to tell him that his money has dried up and his staff is gone other than a few loyal people left. We're running on fumes and unless this merger goes through, there won't even be anything for him to come back to.

He already lost everything once before. Back when my mom died, and our home went into fore-closure. He rebuilt from the ground up. Like most that go through poverty and homelessness, the recovery process took well over a decade. But he did it. He was finally starting to see the reward for his years of hard work and sacrifice.

Until the Abernathy family got greedy.

My hand tightens around the phone as a familiar

surge of anger fills me. I'd love to lash out at them. But I'd be nothing more than a dog nipping at their heels. No, I have to be patient and bide my time. That means going through with this sham of a marriage, no matter how repulsive I find my groom.

"I have to go now, Dad," I tell him, my throat tight. Is he ever going to forgive me? What if he gets out of jail and realizes what's happened?

No, I won't let that happen. By the time my father is released, and the charges are dropped, everything will be back to normal. Except that his company will be gone. At least, his ideas will be.

But it doesn't matter. We can rebuild again, and I can get even with the Abernathy family. I can destroy them from the inside out.

After we say our goodbyes, I take a deep breath and survey my appearance one last time. I've been waxed, tweezed, and plucked in every conceivable place on my body. I've been lotioned and perfumed, had my hair and makeup done. Finally, I've been squeezed into a dress that's a white monstrosity.

Now there's only one thing left to do before the ceremony. It's time for the first look. Some magical event where the bride and groom see each other for the first time. The thought sends a wave of bile up my throat, but I choke it back. I will not give

Andrew the satisfaction of knowing he disgusts me. He's a sexist jerk who eyes me with open hostility. Our marriage will be anything but a happy union.

I should probably call one of the annoying bridesmaids that my new mother-in-law hired but I can't bring myself to do it. Instead, I gather the skirt of this hideous dress and walk the ten steps across the hall from the bridal suite to the large room where the first look is supposed to take place.

To my relief, I find the space empty. It gives me a few moments alone to gather my messy emotions. I remind myself that even though this isn't my dream wedding, it doesn't matter.

Eventually, my dad will be out of jail, and I'll divorce Andrew. I'll find a man that really loves me. One who will celebrate my curves and love my big body. He'll laugh at my jokes and listen to me talk about what's happening in the latest alien smut books I'm reading.

He'll find my yoga pants sexy and spin me around when Sinatra comes on the oldies station. But most of all, he'll love me, and we'll have a magical marriage, just like my parents did.

"Yeah, I won't give up. Not ever, dad," I whisper to my reflection in the mirror just as the door swings open.

I brace myself for Andrew and his obnoxious friends. But it's not him. It's a man that looks like Andrew. Except instead of being lean and lithe, this man is big and beefy. A long, full beard covers his face, and his gray blue eyes rake over me with curiosity.

Although he's dressed in a tailored suit that perfectly hugs his large body, showing off broad shoulders and thick thighs, he doesn't look the part of an Abernathy. He's not polished with styled eyebrows and a close shave. He doesn't smell of expensive colognes or have soft hands.

No, this man looks like he's been running through the forest all day, and someone plucked him out of it and stuffed him in a suit. But they didn't bother to try to tame his messy hair that's tied at the nape of his neck or smooth the callouses on his hands. They didn't shape those eyebrows into a perfect arch or demand he trim the curly beard. Something about the feral, untamed look calls to me. Makes me long to throw myself in his arms and beg him to carry me far, far away from here.

It finally clicks in my brain that this must be Andrew's little brother. What was his name again? Andrew mentioned it once. Laughed about his brother being some silent mountain man before he launched into what I could only assume was a mocking imitation of a man barely able to speak.

I adjust my veil, trying to act uninterested by his presence, even as my stomach tightens. My heart races, and I fight to keep my breathing even. Why is it suddenly so hot in here? Why does the room feel so small now that the mountain man is in here?

He looks like he wants to say something. He licks his full bottom lip and opens his mouth. But nothing comes out. Why I'm disappointed that I don't get to hear the gruff stranger's voice, I don't know.

Instead, I force a smile and step forward. If I'm going to destroy these people from the inside out, I need to play nice. "Hi, I'm Cadence."

He nods at me. I'm still disappointed that he hasn't let me hear his voice. Is it deep and growly, as unrefined and gruff as he is?

"It's nice to meet the last member of the family." I clutch my wedding dress, like that will somehow remind my traitorous body that this is not my groom. "Your family is very nice."

He puts a hand on my shoulder, his touch searing me even through the thin material of the wedding dress. He's branding me without a word, making me long to be his. For a moment, I could swear that I see attraction flash in his gaze.

But then the door is swinging open again and he's already snatched away his hand.

Andrew swaggers into the room, his usual entourage behind him. I don't think the man sneezes without an audience. After all, his fragile ego needs constant applause and frequent strokes.

The thought of consummating with this vile man-child is repulsive. But one icky night and then it will be over. I will not give Jack Abernathy any ammunition to say it wasn't a real marriage.

"Oh, good. You met her," Andrew slurs. He's drunk again. He's usually drunk, and truthfully, I don't care.

I turn back to the mirror and pretend to fuss over my appearance rather than give him an ounce of my attention. But in the mirror's reflection, my gaze goes to his brother. He reaches for Andrew's sloppy tie as if he's the older brother.

"She's a fuckin' hippo," Andrew complains.

I ignore the comment. I already know that Andrew finds my body revolting. He hasn't once hidden his disgust over this marriage or his contempt for my body. He thinks I'm some poor maiden that's lucky to be blessed with a gem like him. In his mind, I should be grateful for any scrap of affection he throws my way.

Well, I'm not desperate and I'm not grateful. I'm in love with my curves and one day, I'll find a man that loves them too.

"Put her fat ass on a diet," one of the groomsmen suggests. He's dealing cards. Andrew always has a game going. A chronic gambler, it's little wonder that his parents dole out cash to him. They're giving him a large payday for going through with this wedding and he gets a stipend for every month he stays married to me.

"Everyone knows that whales don't diet," a different groomsman says. I forget his name, but he's the one who propositioned me at our engagement party. Yeah, Andrew's friends are real winners.

I risk another covert glance at Andrew's brother. Beneath his bushy beard, his jaw is tight, and his hands are clenched into fists. He's not really angry, is he? Surely, he knows what his brother and his friends are like.

"Hey, Cadence," Andrew smirks. He told me once that he has a look that can get any woman to drop her panties in thirty seconds. I think that might be what he's trying to give me now but if so, he's found the one woman immune to his charm. "Can whales even orgasm?"

# 3
## CADENCE

BEFORE I CAN EVEN BLINK—LET ALONE RESPOND—
Andrew is on the floor. His brother is on top of him,
punching him repeatedly.

I gasp, as shock floods through me. I've never had
anyone defend me like that. Let alone, a strange man
that I barely know.

Two of Andrew's friends finally manage to yank
the mountain man off and my groom crawls out
from under his brother's large frame. Fire dances in
his eyes but I don't miss the slight tremble to his
hand when he tips his head back and pinches his
nose closed.

This can't be about me. It has to be about some
unresolved issues between the brothers. They don't'
even know me.

"What the hell is your problem? Is your brain still scrambled, you dumb mute?" Andrew demands.

Is that why he's barely said a word? Could it be that he wasn't being unfriendly earlier but that he has difficulty communicating?

His chest is still heaving from the exertion of throwing punches. His bloodied knuckles are rapidly turning a deep shade of violet. But it's the wild look in his eyes that has my heart skipping a beat. He grounds out a word. It's so low and deep, as if the effort is taking everything from him. "Mine."

"Wait. You want lardo?" Andrew asks.

He nods at his brother, a fierce look on his face. I think they're doing this. I think they're actually negotiating for me. But why would the brutal mountain man want me? More than that, why did he defend me?

"Oh, this is too good. The whale and the idiot." He snatches tissues from his groomsman and shoves them up his nostrils.

I open my mouth. I should say something here. The deal with Jack only mentioned Andrew. He never said something about having another son or about marrying him instead. Even if I think that maybe this hulking man in front of me might be a better husband, I still can't risk the terms of the deal.

I have to get my dad out of jail, no matter what it takes.

Andrew seems to think over this for a moment before he says, "Tell you what, little bro. You can have her. But you handle mom and dad."

Savage satisfaction crosses his brother's expression and I shiver. I'm not afraid of this big man in front of me. I'm afraid of the excited pull low in my belly and the way he makes my heart speed up with a single look.

Andrew issues commands to his assistant, clearly grateful to be done with me. He must really hate me if he's willing to let go of the payday his parents were about to deposit in his account. But I can't bring myself to feel hurt or upset. Instead, all I feel is deep relief. Like I've just escaped a near collision.

"You and tubby have fun making little piglets," Andrew's parting shot is nasally thanks to the damage to his face.

His brother takes one step toward the door. That's all he has to do. The slightest shift of his weight on his feet and Andrew and the other groomsmen are shoving each other out of the way. The man in front of me might be the little brother, but he's clearly an alpha.

He nods to himself when they're all gone then

turns to me. His movements are slow when he holds out his hand. His knuckles are bruised for me. He fought for me, to keep me out of a marriage with a cruel man. He speaks now, once again sounding like his vocal chords have been scraped with gravel. "Marry. Me."

If there were ever a moment to back out of the deal with the Abernathy family, this is it. If I had an ounce of self-preservation, maybe I would. Instead, I take his hand in mine. Just like that, I jump from the frying pan into the fire.

———

THIRTY MINUTES. THAT'S HOW LONG IT TOOK FOR THE Abernathy parents to switch out the grooms. I don't know what was said or what deals were made behind the scenes, but I went to Jack. I made sure my arrangement with him was still in place.

He regarded me through the hazy smoke of a cigar and assured me that this was a better idea than anything he could have dreamed up. I don't know what that means, but I don't care. As long as my father is set free and the fake charges against him are dropped.

I also finally got the name of my groom. Brennon, a name that means prince. But he doesn't carry himself like one. No, my soon-to-be husband carries himself like a king, a man who owns everything and fears nothing. He answers to no one and rules all he desires.

By the time the wedding ceremony is taking place, his suit is miraculously clear from his brother's blood and his hands are patched up. He's easily the most imposing man in the room, standing in front of the altar and waiting to pledge his devotion to me.

Our gazes connect and for a moment I forget to breathe. There's only him and me in this cathedral.

He clasps my hand in his calloused one. Andrew had baby soft hands that were perfectly manicured. My man has dirt under his nails and for some crazy reason, it makes me want to trust him.

When the officiant asks Brennon if he takes me as his wife, he keeps his voice quiet. I'm pretty sure he murmured something about ice cream. Even if he did, it never shows on the officiant's face. He breezes right on by as if everything is normal. But I see the frustration flicker across Brennon's face before he hides it.

I squeeze his hand in return, wanting him to know it's OK. I'd be frustrated if I struggled to talk too. Suddenly, I remember the way Andrew mocked his brother's inability to speak. I thought he was making fun of the fact that he was from the mountains. Now that I know the truth, anger burns in me.

Brennon might be my enemy, but he deserves to be treated like a person. He deserves respect and kindness.

The officiant announces that it's time to kiss the bride then my groom is leaning in. I brace myself for the kind of sloppy, aggressive kiss that would come from Andrew. But this is different.

Brennon's lips are gentle against mine and he cups the back of my head, deepening the kiss. I forget about everything when his tongue sweeps into my mouth. About the wedding and our audience and my dad's problems. There's only Brennon, sweetly stroking my tongue and making a soft groan. My nipples harden to sharp points and my panties go damp as I imagine what his tongue would feel like on other areas of my body.

It's over too soon. He pulls away, his blue eyes glittering as he stares down at me. Arousal and desire and something I can't define mix in his gaze. Relief fills me at knowing I'm not the only one affected so deeply.

We're announced as man and wife while I stand

frozen in place. This isn't like I thought it would be. I thought the world would feel as if it were ending. But it feels like my world was in gray and is now in brilliant hues of color. All thanks to the sexy mountain man beside me.

Brennon puts a hand on my back. The heat from his skin burns through the thin material of my dress and I look to him. He gives the slightest nod before guiding me down the aisle as all of the high society people applaud us.

Wedding pictures are next, and I spend the next hour in my fancy dress and my high heels that are worth a small fortune. It's strange to me to think that some people live this way. I could buy a luxury car for what these custom designed shoes cost.

The wedding planner has spent our entire shoot hassling the photographers and making sure the lighting is just right. She finally turns her barracuda gaze on me. "Ten minutes to change before you'll be in the limo and on your way to the reception hall."

I've just been granted a reprieve, and I don't have to be told twice. Gathering up my skirts, I hurry toward the bridal suite. I'm blessedly alone and close my eyes in relief. All I want is to change into my faded yoga pants, grab a cup of steaming tea, and get lost in a smutty romance.

But that's not happening today so I square my shoulders. I remind myself that I'm doing this for my father. That I'll find a way to get through this marriage with Brennon. Although after that kiss, I'm not so sure that our marriage will be a hardship.

I manage to extricate myself from the dress but just barely. I thought I would have to call for help but by some miracle, I got free. I glance at my reflection in the mirror. My white lace bra does nothing to hide my sharp nipples.

For just a moment, I consider sliding my fingers between my thighs, I'm already swollen. It wouldn't take much for me to satiate this hunger. All those moments with Andrew and never once did I feel anything stir. But one look from sexy Brennon and my panties turn to ash.

As if he knows I'm thinking about him, there's a loud, authoritative knock on the door then my handsome husband is barreling through. I love the way that tuxedo jacket is too tight around his arms and shoulders, like he's about to bust the seams at any moment.

"What are you doing here?" I ask with a slight tremor in my voice. But it isn't fear because I make no move to cover myself. I want him to look. More than that, I want him to like what he sees.

"Mine," he growls. The single word sends a bolt between my thighs, and I squeeze my legs together.

He sees me squirm and stalks across the room. He sweeps me into his arms. Next thing I know, I'm pinned between the wall and his hard body. His manhood is digging into my hip, and I know I don't imagine the feral glint in his gaze.

"You're the enemy," I whisper right before his lips are nuzzling my neck, his beard teasing my sensitive skin. But even as I call him my enemy, I know the real truth. I belong to this mountain man.

4

# BRENNON

SHE SMELLS LIKE HONEY AND VANILLA. AS I NUZZLE her neck, I feel as if I've found what I've been looking for. I didn't even know something was missing from my life. Until her.

"You're the enemy," she whispers.

I don't know what that means or why she thinks that way. But right now, I don't care. All I want is this beautiful woman in my bed. I have to see her spread out, waiting and willing and wet. I have to feel her against me, the glide of our two bodies becoming one.

"Home," I murmur against her skin.

She pulls away from me and looks up. "Home?" She repeats the word with a question in her voice and frowns.

I tap my chest, indicating I want to take her to mine.

She uses my distraction to step around me. She reaches for a pretty dress. Something green that makes her flushed cheeks look even prettier. I didn't know a blush could be arousing. But with her, it is. Everything about her calls to me, pulls me in like a riptide. I'm drowning and I don't want to be rescued.

"Home. My stuff is all at Andrew's penthouse," she murmurs as she smooths down the skirt of the pretty dress.

The idea of her things being in his place is enough to make me snap. Her things don't belong at his place. They should be at mine. It should be my kitchen counters where her keys and sunglasses are scattered. It should be my sink that her dishes are in. It should be my floor that her clothes are on.

With a growl, I stride across the room and pick her up. I throw her over my shoulder with ease. She might be curvy but she's a petite little thing. The perfect size for me to carry around whenever I want. The thought fills me with satisfaction. Yeah, this is how things should be.

"What are you doing?" She demands. Her voice sounds funny, probably because she's inverted, and all the blood is rushing to her head.

I just grunt again, the tightness in my chest only easing once I've deposited her in the front of my car. I make quick work of the seatbelt, strapping in the most precious thing I've ever owned in my life. I've got to figure out a way to make this woman fall in love with me and quick.

"Suitcases," she says. She points to the limo parked around the side of the church. My parents are going to shit when they realize we're gone, but I don't care. I want time alone with my new bride. Her gaze softens, and she promises, "I'll still be here."

I grab three suitcases I know have to be hers. They're not masculine like Andrew's and more than that, they're worn. Not the luxury brand stuff that a wife of her status should be using. The thought fills me with relief. It's one more reminder that I made the right decision by taking her from him.

The drive to Courage County seems longer than normal with her sweet scent filling the car and making my cock press painfully against the zipper of my slacks.

I should say something, tell her about the little town she's moving to. The words don't come easily. Instead, I grunt and point to the places that she might like. Downtown isn't large, but it is beautiful with the snow-covered shops and icicle covered awnings in the early evening light.

Along the sidewalks, children pelt each other with snowballs and neighbors call out to one another. Courage is more than just a town, it's a whole community. A place where everyone is safe and welcome. As soon as my friend, Nash told me that, I knew it was where I wanted to be.

Even now, I don't leave my cabin much to go into town but that doesn't matter. Everyone still greets me with enthusiasm and kindness. No one acts like I'm strange because I communicate mainly in grunts. They're the kind of folks that accept you as you are. The world could use more of these places.

Cadence is quiet on our ride through town, and I can't help but wonder what she's thinking. I want to know every thought in her head. Every thought she's ever had and every thought she will have. I want to know everything about the curvy woman in the seat next to me.

But I don't try to ask. It's enough for now that she's here with me, willingly beside me. *Except that she called you the enemy.*

I'll have to work to learn to communicate with her. Before now, I was never much interested in communicating with other people. I didn't have to be told that the Abernathy family would be embarrassed to have a son using sign language. It would be admitting to a disability, a flaw.

But it surprises me just how much I want to communicate with my new wife. I want to know everything about her, but I also want her to know everything about me. I don't want there to ever be anything between us.

Finally, my car finishes the long chug up the winding mountain road and my cabin is in view. My gut tightens. It's one of the fancier cabins here but by the Abernathy standards, it's a shack. Will she hate it? I need her to love it here, to love being with me.

She stares at the cabin for a long moment when I cut off the car and I wish she'd say something. Anything.

But she makes no remark as she opens the front door. She barely glances around at my sparsely decorated living room that's as sterile as a hospital waiting room. I wish I were the type of person who knew how to make home welcoming and cozy.

She folds her arms across her ample chest, the move pushing her bountiful breasts even higher. "I'm not backing out on the terms of our deal."

I frown, trying to understand her logic. I don't know anything about her deal with my family. But I'm assuming that since this was a business merger, there are terms to fulfill. When I don't say anything, she huffs at me. "Consummation."

It finally dawns on me what she's talking about. For a moment, scenes from my parents' loveless marriage flash in front of my eyes. The pain starts deep in my chest, and I rub at it absently.

I never wanted something like what they had. I never wanted a marriage that felt more like a board-room meeting than two friends navigating life together. But it seems that my woman came into this union with very different expectations. I can't blame her for that when we barely had a chance to talk before the wedding. Still, it doesn't mean I'll agree to her demand so easily. Before I have her body, I want her heart.

With a scowl of my own, I wrap my fingers around her arm and tug her toward the bedroom. This is my bedroom, and there are no other ones in the house. After all, it's not like I was planning for overnight guests when I built this.

I stop at the threshold and turn her toward me. I'd love more than anything to take her up on her offer, but it wouldn't mean anything to her. Despite her open invitation, I press a gentle kiss to her forehead. Then I turn and leave the room without another word.

I don't see her again for the rest of the evening though I can hear her moving around my bedroom. It drives me crazy to know that she's only a few feet away from me. I try to remind myself that Cadence is under my roof. It's not much, but it's a start.

To distract myself, I reach for my phone. I have to find a way to make my new wife fall in love with me fast. Quickly, I type in my search query. *How to make a woman fall in love with you.*

Too late, I realize my error. I didn't type those words into my phone's search function. Instead, I typed those words into the group chat with my friends. Nash is the first to respond. *What are you? Fourteen?*

He's only a mile or two down the road. He's blind which means all of his messages are sent with assistive technology. Sometimes, we tease him about the dumb things his phone autocorrects. But he just laughs it off with the rest of us.

Romans replies next. *Stalk her.*

I don't think Roman is joking. There's a girl in

town that he's head over heels for and yet he's never made a move. It might have something to do with his prison record. I'm not exactly sure what he was in for, and I've never asked.

Trace is the last to get back to me. *Tell her she's yours.*

Trace turns his metal welding creations into art that he sells. He's actually pretty good at it. I know his family owns a ranch in another state. But he doesn't talk about it. Just moved out to the mountains one day.

I fire off a quick text of my own, feeling my frustration mount. *Any real advice?*

Roman: *Stalk her some more. Learn everything you can about her.*

Of course, he'd say that. The guy probably thinks it's the same thing as dating a woman. Not that Gabby, the petite mechanic in town, seems to mind his attention.

Nash: *Learn what she likes. Then do nice stuff for her.*

Trace: *Sit her down and tell her she's yours. Problem solved.*

It's obvious my fellow mountain men aren't likely to become relationship experts any time soon. Still, the idea of finding out what she likes isn't a bad one. It takes me a moment to figure out how I can do some recon on my girl. Maybe she has a social media account or two. If I'm lucky, I'll find what I need to woo my new bride.

5

CADENCE

I don't understand Brennon. I thought when I offered to consummate the marriage, he would want it too. I know he's attracted to me. Or at least he wants me if the way his bulge was digging into my hip in the bridal suite was any indication. He kept putting his lips on my neck and growling under his breath.

When we arrived at his cabin, he sent me to the bedroom, kissed me on the forehead, and left me alone for the rest of the night. From what I can tell of the bedroom, it appeared to be his room. Maybe I spent most of the night combing through his drawers and his things looking for clues to who he was.

I know from what I've managed to piece together

from Andrew and his parents that Brennon used to be the CEO of the family company, but something happened to make him step back. Does this mean that Brennon was able to speak at some point? And if he was, what happened that changed him?

After a sleepless night pondering these things, I take a quick shower in the bedroom suite and put on my usual yoga pants and t-shirt. The best part of running a company with my father was the option to wear comfortable clothes. I skip the makeup and move to the kitchen where I can hear the sounds of someone moving about.

Brennon didn't mention having a housekeeper. But then again, we didn't really talk last night. I didn't think to ask him any questions. I was too tired and too overwhelmed by the day we'd had.

When I come into the kitchen, I'm momentarily struck by just how beautiful my husband is. The button-down plaid shirt is stretched tight across his back and when he moves, the material pulls tight across his broad shoulders. His blue jeans are sculpted to his firm ass, and he turns when he hears me enter the room.

His hair is loose, free from the ponytail it was in yesterday. His thick brown locks dust his shoulders. I have the sudden urge to run my fingers through it, to tug on it as he kisses me passionately. What would his beard feel like against my skin again?

He lifts his eyebrows and I realize that I've been caught staring at my new husband.

"Did you sleep well?" I manage to stammer out.

He gives me a brief nod then tips his head. For a moment, I think maybe he's asking me the same question in return.

"Me, too," I'm quick to answer, even though the words are a lie. I barely slept. Not only was it weird being in an unfamiliar place, but being married to Brennon is slightly unnerving, too. I have no idea what to expect from this hunky mountain man. Is this even a real marriage in his eyes?

He pushes a plate of food into my hands. I accept it and glance up at him, surprised by the concern I see in his eyes.

I'm normally a muffin and black coffee kind of girl for breakfast, but there's something about the way he's looking at me. It feels nice to be taken care of. I know that Andrew would never deign to do a task like making me breakfast.

I take a seat at the table and bite into a piece of crunchy bacon. I give him a nod that has his expression softening into a smile. It's strange to see

Brennon smile. When he does, his whole face lights up.

He settles at the table with a plate of his own.

I can't help but ask him what his plans are for our honeymoon. I stumble over the word honeymoon, uncertain of what it means since we haven't defined our marriage.

He stops chewing to stare at me.

Instantly, I feel self-conscious and wonder if I shouldn't have asked that question. Quickly, I amend my question, "I mean, this is fun."

I don't want him thinking that I was expecting some lavish vacation. Andrew and I had planned a stay in Cancún that I wasn't even looking forward to. I'd much rather be cozy in my new husband's cabin than to be with Andrew on a sunny beach.

He reaches across the table and takes my hand, giving it a gentle squeeze before he manages to ground out, "I…will…make…you…happy."

His words cause my breath to catch in my throat because I know that Andrew never would have worried about my happiness or my comfort. Yet Brennon has done nothing but show concern for me.

We finish our meal together in silence and when we're done, I reach for the dishes. He cooked so it's only fair I help clean up. But before I can load the dishwasher, Brennon takes my hand and tugs me out of the kitchen. I love the feel of his hand wrapping around mine, the way he touches me gently. Like I'm delicate and precious.

I follow after him, curious about what he wants to show me. He leads me down a set of stairs into the basement. I gasp when he pushes through the double doors made of mahogany.

Leather chairs are arranged across from a sofa on an expensive Persian rug that covers the floor. A fireplace in the center of the room has a large impressionist painting hung above it. I don't recognize the piece, but I'd bet good money it's an original. This is the only room in the cabin that's opulent. It speaks to a man who has come from money.

But what I love about the space are the bookshelves. They're built-in against the walls, the same deep mahogany as the doors. Half of the shelves are empty while the other half are filled with books. He must easily own several hundred books, and I can't help wondering if he's read them all.

"This place is beautiful," I breathe.

I step forward and reach for the books. Then I stop myself and turn to Brennon, silently asking for permission. After all, a personal library is something sacred. The fact that he shared his with me means something.

When he nods his approval, I run my fingertips along the spines of a few books. As I do, I note that he's a big fan of mysteries and thrillers. There's some sci-fi mixed in here, too. Space opera books, I suspect.

A small part of me is disappointed to find we don't have any similar tastes. Then again, if Brennon were reading blue alien smut, I'd probably have some questions for him, just like he would have questions for me.

Brennon beams at me, pride clearly written on his face. It's strange to me the way he seems so focused on pleasing me and making me happy.

"You like to read a lot," I say. A pang of sadness hits me in my chest as I wonder if these are the only conversations he's able to have. Brennon lives alone. He has no one to talk with him or ask him about his day. He's alone in the world.

His phone buzzes, and he grins at it. He gestures for me to follow him, and even though I'm hesitant to leave the library with its collection of books, I do follow him.

He moves to the front door where two men in uniform are bringing in heavy boxes. Brennon nods toward one and indicates he wants me to open it.

Curious, I drop to my knees and gently pull apart the flaps. What I see has me breaking into a grin. There are books in here. But not just any books. These are my favorite books. Books I enjoyed in childhood. Books I loved as a teenager. Even my favorite blue alien smut books.

I move to the second box and find more of the same, boxes and boxes of my favorites. Some are even signed author copies while others are first editions. I glance at Brennon to see he's smiling too.

"You got all these for me." I say quietly. He nods and my heart feels too big for my body. This man has swept me off my feet in one gesture, especially when I open another box and find it filled with books from my *to be read* pile.

"How did you know?" I ask.

He pulls his phone from his pocket and shoves it toward me. I look at the screen and see my profile on a popular book tracking website. I use it to rank the books I read and keep track of the ones I haven't read yet.

"Thank you." Before I can stop myself, I lean up and press a soft kiss to his bearded cheek.

He grumbles something, but I can't hear it

because I'm already following the uniformed worker down to the library where he's adding my boxes to the room. My new husband bought me books, and I'm pretty sure I could fall in love with him just for that.

---

*Brennon*

SHE HUMS. CADENCE HUMS AS SHE WORKS. I DIDN'T think I would like to have another person in my space and hear them hum. But being here with Cadence in my library today, I don't mind it.

If anything, it's kind of nice to have another person with me. No, that's not it. What I actually like is having Cadence with me. She fits in my world and in my life. I don't know how I got so lucky that I stumbled in there and found her when I did.

Thank God I came to my brother's wedding. It haunted me all night last night, thoughts of what would have happened had I only sent a wedding gift and not shown up. The only thing that kept me sane was looking down and seeing that gold band on my finger.

Cadence belongs to me. She's mine. She's my

wife, and that means I get to spoil her whenever I want. Starting with giving her a huge library.

She exclaims over all the books as we unpack them. I thought for sure she'd be one of those people who would arrange her book collection by author. But surprisingly, she does it by color.

It takes me a moment, but eventually I can see her pattern. She's following the colors of a rainbow, and I have to admit that it's bright and beautiful. She nudges my side. Her fingertips are warm, and I feel her warmth through the cotton of my plaid button down.

"Can you put this one up there?" She asks.

I do as she instructs, patiently putting the books on the high shelf. She beams at me with every book I put away. Just her smile alone makes me feel ten feet tall. I still can't believe that she said yes when I told her to marry me.

"I didn't have a lot of books as a kid. But my dad would take me every week to the library, and I would load up a backpack full of books. Even though things were hard for us, he taught me that stories can help you discover new worlds and find answers to your problems. But most of all, they can bring you comfort. They remind you that you're not alone. I guess that's why I read so much." She gives a chuckle like she feels self-conscious after her admission.

I touch her shoulder and nod wanting her to know I understand her loneliness. Before the stroke, the only thing I ever read were business books by the gurus of the year that talked about how to hustle harder and crush your goals.

After my stroke, even the tiniest of tasks were difficult. That's when I discovered the world of fiction. I couldn't move from the bed without assistance, but I could be a commander on a space-ship, or I could be behind enemy lines, fighting for my life. Those books helped me with my recovery just as much as my physical therapy and medication.

"Favorite?" I manage the question, hating the gravelly sound of my voice. I might be able to speak, but I don't do it often. Too much hassle so now when I do talk, my voice sounds odd even to my own ears.

She looks around the library and shakes her head.

"There are too many, but maybe I would start with this one." She picks up a book with a blue alien on the front, but it's clear from his ripped abs and piercing gaze that this isn't one of the space opera books I read. No, this looks more like some type of romance.

I reach for it, curious as to her taste.

She snatches it away. "What are you doing?"

I make a gesture to indicate I want to read it.

She looks between me and the book, a slight pink tinge to her cheeks. "You want to read my romance book?"

If it has anything to do with Cadence, I want to know about it. I want to learn more about what turns her on and gets her going. If that's what's in those pages, I definitely want to see it.

"Why?" Cadence squeaks.

I reach for my phone in my pocket, frustrated with my inability to do more than utter a word or two. It's all there in my head. I can see all of the words plainly. I can even write most sentences clearly. I just can't seem to get them out.

The doctors told me that happens with some types of aphasia, but it doesn't matter if I can still communicate through writing. It's damn frustrating to have to take the time to spell out what I want. Usually, I don't bother, but with Cadence, I want her to know what I'm thinking.

On my phone, I type out a quick message. *I want to know what turns you on.*

She looks again to the book, then finally shoves it in my hands. "Page sixty."

She grabs an armful of books from the box and begins quickly sorting them on a shelf. She's not looking at me, which tells me she's embarrassed. A gentleman would probably wait and read it alone, but I don't. Now that I'm this close to figuring out what excites my new bride, I have to know.

"You can't read it now," she exclaims when she realizes what I'm doing, but I don't listen to her.

I hold the book out of her reach and continue reading. I don't have a tail, but I can definitely do some of this stuff with her.

For the first time in my life, I'm glad that I was never interested in having a woman. I always avoided romantic entanglements for fear I'd end up exactly like my parents with their cold, heartless marriage. I wanted something warm, someone to come home to. Now with Cadence, I've found her.

"Brennon," she calls my name, a slight pout marring her beautiful features. I find I like the look of those full lips in a pout.

I continue reading the scene. This is arousing as fuck. My cock presses painfully against my pants as I read about the hero feasting on the heroine's pussy. I'm not willing to go all the way with her, but there are definitely things we can do while I wait for her heart to become mine.

As I finish reading the scene, I reach for my phone again. I type out a quick message. "Do you want me to do this to you?"

I didn't think it was possible, but my girl's blush deepens even more. She finally shrugs a shoulder and says, "Maybe. If you want to."

My thumbs fly across my phone's keyboard. "Hell yeah, I want to."

6

CADENCE

THIS IS THE MOMENT I SHOULD TELL HIM. TELL HIM I'm completely inexperienced. I've only ever read about this stuff. Sure, I've put my hand between my thighs a few times. Even managed an orgasm or two.

But I've never dated or had a boyfriend. My life has been complicated. My father and I were often homeless except for a few times when we were lucky enough to crash on someone's couch for a few days. There were shelters, but we usually didn't stay at those very long. They're not always safe, especially for a young girl. My dad knew our car—even on the nights we couldn't afford to heat it—was still the best option.

Instead of dating boys or worrying about prom, I was focused on survival. It all paid off because by the time I graduated high school, we were getting back on our feet.

We had a crappy apartment. I was waitressing during the day and taking online marketing courses at night. My dad got a job as a night janitor and one magical moment, we went from barely scraping by to millionaires. Even now, I still find it surreal to step into a grocery store and have the option to fill a cart with everything I need.

"You want to do the stuff in there?" I ask again to clarify because this is so strange to me. I'm married now. Married to a very hot man who is offering to explore one of my favorite fantasies. "W-with me?"

Instead of answering, he pulls me into his arms and carries me to the leather couch. He sets me down gently and pauses to brush strands of hair that have come loose from my ponytail.

He drops to his knees in front of the couch and cups my face. The intensity in his gaze has me barely breathing. He wants me. Brennon definitely wants me.

To my surprise, he doesn't push me down and just start licking me the way the hero did in the book. Instead, he kisses me. Softly and gently exploring my mouth with his tongue.

I wind my fingers through his hair, pulling him

closer. His hair is just as soft and silky as I imagined it'd be. He growls when I give it a light tug and nips at my bottom lip.

He presses kisses along my jaw before he nuzzles my neck again. His beard tickles my skin, and I can't help giggling at the sensation.

Brennon pulls away to glance at me and I quickly explain, "Your beard. I like the way it feels against my skin."

I stroke it with my other hand. He's all hard lines and muscle everywhere but he's soft here.

His eyes crinkle at the corners. It strikes me then that there no laugh lines on his face. No evidence he's spent years enjoying and loving life. "Tell me about yourself."

"Later," he murmurs before going back to kiss my neck again. He trails his kisses lower and lower until pulling up my t-shirt. He stares at my bra in concentration and the look on his face has me wanting to melt into the cushions right there. He's so sexy when he's serious. He flicks open the clasp, and cool air rushes over my breasts as he bares me.

He wastes no time. He lowers his head, sucking one of my tight buds into his mouth.

I moan at the sensation. It feels so right to have

his lips on me, sucking and nipping at my skin. Bringing me pleasure.

He spends long moments feasting on me and the entire time, he's growling. I don't know why but those possessive noises he makes only fuel my need. My panties are growing damp and I squeeze my thighs together, trying to get some of the friction I need. But it's still not enough. I need more. I need Brennon there.

I whimper his name. "Lower."

He lets go of my breast with a wet pop and takes a moment to stare down at me. The way he's focused, it's like he's trying to commit this moment to memory. Like it matters to him. But it can't matter to him. It can't matter to me. This is a business deal. All we're doing is confirming it. The thought causes a hollow ache in my chest I don't fully understand.

He leans down again, trailing his lips and fingers across my stomach. Every kiss is gentle, and every touch is reverent. He worships the cellulite and adores the bumps. There's not an area of my tummy that he isn't lavishing with attention.

Then he moves to the waistband of my yoga pants. He glances up at me one more time, as if confirming I want this.

I nod, my cheeks warm and my pussy so swollen that it's painful. Everything in me craves this man's tongue on my skin, lapping at my folds and drinking my juices.

He pulls my pants and panties down, tossing them onto the floor. Despite my arousal, I start to close my legs. It's too much. Too vulnerable.

But Brennon doesn't let me hide. He pries my legs apart. He's gentle but insistent, refusing to let me cover myself from his gaze. In that deep, gravelly voice, he says, "Love. The. View."

His words have me relaxing into the couch. He's been nothing but kind and reverent with my body. Sometimes, he looks like he can't quite believe he's getting to touch me.

He maneuvers my legs until my feet are flat on the sofa and my knees are in the air. Then he wedges his broad shoulders between my thighs. He parts my pussy lips as I stare at the ceiling and will myself to relax into the moment.

With anyone else, this wouldn't be a big deal. But this is Brennon, my husband. The man who saved me from months, maybe even years of misery. He stepped in when he didn't have to, and he's been nothing but a gentleman.

The first slide of his tongue over my folds brings

me back into the moment. There's no way I can think about anything else when it feels so good to have his tongue there. He licks me a few more times, pausing to look up at me occasionally. That's when I realize what he's doing. He's experimenting, trying to decide what I enjoy.

"I like it when you do it like that," I tell him with the next pass of his tongue. He rolls it against my slick center and that's my favorite thing.

He does it again and again until more moisture gushes from my pussy. We're making a mess on his fancy leather sofa and the sounds of his big tongue against my drenched folds are obscene. But the knowledge only sends me higher, especially when he inserts one thick finger into my aching channel. That's when I sigh in relief. I hadn't even realized I was craving the sensation of being filled until he did that.

He thrusts in and out and for a moment, I let myself wish it were his cock. I wish he were above me, panting my name and telling me that I belong to him.

His tongue finds my clit at the same time he adds a second finger. I clench my pussy, unable to hold back the spasm. He's giving me too many wonderful sensations at once. Tingles race down my spine, and I gasp his name again when he circles my clit again.

Brennon seems to know what I need because he never breaks his rhythm. He keeps licking and sucking and thrusting, giving me everything my body needs to soar higher and higher. When the orgasm hits, it knocks the breath from my lungs and for a moment I can't see anything. There's only the feeling of my husband giving me this exquisite pleasure.

Even as I float back down, he continues to pleasure me. His pace is lazier, slower this time. Despite the orgasm I just had, another immediately begins building. I'm so sensitive that I thread my fingers through his hair. "Too much."

"One more," he commands, his voice laced with a plea. He wants me to have this as much as I do, wants to watch me come apart in pleasure again.

He continues to work my body until I'm spasming, gushing into his beard and crying out his name. My body is covered in sweat, and I've never been so energized and exhausted at the same time.

He gives me a soft smile, leaning forward to cup my face in his hand. The look of tenderness in his expression is what has the warning bells in my head going off. *We shouldn't be doing this.*

I push myself up to my elbows, pulling away from his touch. I don't look at him. I don't want to know if this meant something to him. Because it can't. It can't mean anything.

"We can't do this," I murmur as I stand. The air in the room is cold without pants. I grab mine and quickly pull them on before I pause to fasten my bra and my shirt. Then I leave the library because suddenly the room is too small, and I can't focus on anything other than the way the walls are closing in.

I race to the front of the house, stepping onto the front porch. My bare feet recoil at the cold planks, but I welcome the sting of pain.

"This was not part of the deal," I whisper as I watch big, fat snowflakes drift lazily toward the ground. Catching feelings for my new husband wasn't part of the deal at all.

# 7
## BRENNON

I BLINK AT THE COUCH, TRYING TO COMPREHEND WHAT just happened. My woman enjoyed that. I could see how much she did. Hell, I could feel it when she came on my fingers. The way her pussy squeezed me so tightly had me coming in my pants.

I adjust my jeans and search the house. I finally find my wife on the porch. She's not wearing shoes or a coat. I should spank her ass. It's too damn cold for her to be in the snow without protection.

With a scowl, I grab the items for her. I join her on the porch, covering her shoulders with the coat. Then I put my big work boots down in front of her. I nudge her and she puts her pink-polished toes in them.

Finally, she sends me a look of pure misery. I

couldn't have been that bad at it. Probably need some practice. Years of only getting my hand mean I don't quite know what I'm doing with a partner. But instinct seemed to take over when I was with her.

"We can't do this, Brennon," she says. "I can't fall in love with you."

*Love.* The word is a punch to the gut. Does this mean she could develop feelings for me? I was prepared to wait a lifetime for her. But maybe this means she's starting to fall for me.

I reach for her, wanting my arms around her. I need to feel her against me, feel the steady thrum of her heartbeat and know she's falling for me too.

But she sidesteps my arms and lets out a soft sigh. "We'll consummate our marriage, but it can't ever mean anything. It's not a real marriage."

I can't breathe at her words. The hell it's not. This is the realest thing I've ever had in my life and I'm not giving up on it without a fight. First, I need to figure out what's holding her back so I can reassure her I'm here for the long-term.

I have to concentrate all my effort to figure out how to say the word. I can see it in my head, but it doesn't come out. "Yak."

When I was a kid learning the alphabet, the flash-card for the letter *Y* had a yak on it. Since the stroke,

I find myself saying it sometimes when I want to ask the question. It frustrates the hell out of me, and I feel the flush start on my neck. She's the last person I want to sound like an idiot in front of. It killed me that I couldn't even manage our vows. All I could mutter was ice cream.

She doesn't laugh at me the way my brother would. She doesn't make fun of me like my father. She doesn't even look embarrassed the way my mom does. She just quiets and waits for me. When I don't say anything, she whispers gently, "Try again."

It'll just come out the same way again. I know my brain and once I get frustrated, the words can't be untangled.

She wraps her arms around herself while she waits. She's draped in my jacket and if we weren't discussing this, I'd find it arousing. After several long minutes pass without me trying to clarify what I said, she says, "Look, it's OK. You don't have to justify yourself in any of this. I think, maybe it's possible that you didn't even know about my father. At least, I hope not." She shivers then. "We should go in. It's cold out here."

I don't know what she means about her father. I'm not looped into anything with the business anymore. The moment my father realized I could no longer communicate, he stripped the business from me. Even now, he no longer includes me in any business decisions. The company could be burning to the ground, and I wouldn't even know it.

She moves into the house, retreating into the bedroom. I watch her go with a dull ache in the pit of my stomach. I want everything with this woman, and it figures that my family has already fucked it up before I even get a chance to prove to her that we could have something special.

Hurrying to the library where the air still smells of sex, I grab my phone and send a text to the group chat. I'm talking to Roman, the guy who believes stalking a woman is the way to her heart. *Get hacker to research terms of Drew's marriage.*

Roman: *Expensive.*

Me: *Don't care. My wife is worth it.*

As soon as I send the message, I realize that I didn't tell my friends I got married yesterday. They're likely to have a million questions, the gossiping old women. I shut my phone off, so I don't have to answer them.

Unfortunately, that doesn't mean I can dodge their questions. Because an hour later, the three of them show up on my porch.

Cadence answers the door before I can stop her,

and they stare at her without a word. They're big, burly guys, but she doesn't back down. Instead, she gives them a smile. I hate it when she smiles at other men. She should only be allowed to smile at me. That needs to be one of the terms of our marriage. "We're not buying anything today."

Each of them holds something. Nash has a cake. Trace has one of his metal art pieces. Roman has a dish set with a bright red bow on it. That's when I realize the guys are groomed. They've brushed their beards and put on real clothes and made an actual effort.

"Friends," I manage the word to Cadence, so she doesn't keep thinking they're here to sell her something.

"What does his wife look like?" Nash asks.

"Real pretty." Roman gives her a wolfish smile, and I know the bastard. He's trying to irritate me. He's not interested in anyone but that petite girl down at the auto shop.

She glances at me, clearly not sure what to make of the group.

I shake my head to let her know they're joking.

"She's a ten," Trace answers, getting in on the jabs. I'm going to kill these motherfuckers as soon as we're out of Cadence's sight.

Her blush deepens. Dammit, I want to be the only reason she ever blushes.

"We brought wedding gifts," Nash says. "We can give them to you here in the freezing cold…"

I summon my words, searching for the way to tell them to fuck off. Figures the most important expression in the world would evade me at a moment like this.

"Oh, that's sweet. Come in." Cadence gestures for them to step into the living room.

"Two steps up," Roman reminds them. He's used to being the eyes when the four of us go hiking on the mountain.

Nash gets it easy enough. He's blind but his cane lets him figure things out pretty quick. It's Trace that takes a second longer to manage it. He can see, but his hip and leg are messed up. He doesn't walk right. Just sort of teeters everywhere he goes. Best I've managed to put together, he was in a childhood accident that affected his ability to walk. He's in pain most of the time, but I've never seen the man complain. No matter how far we hike.

He's the first to offer his gift to her, a horse sculpture made of metal. He shoves it at her, only grunting, "Wedding gift."

She beams at him. "This is beautiful. I collect horses."

Nash offers the cake. "Figured food is always a safe bet."

"It is," she confirms with a soft smile. This is what I love about this woman. She's kind and gracious, accepting my friends with ease. I could never imagine my family accepting these rough guys without a raised eyebrow or sarcastic remark.

"Can't eat food without dishes," Roman adds, passing her the box with his gnarled hands. He started a construction company after getting out of prison and he used to do a lot of the work himself. But the arthritis that's attacked his hands mean he's stuck managing most of the projects now instead of building things like he loves.

"That's an excellent point," she says. "Why don't I cut into this, and we'll have some slices?"

I grunt my disapproval at her offer. I want all of her attention and her time.

Roman and Trace exchange a look. Nash rubs the back of his neck. "We don't want to impose now."

She waves them into the kitchen, telling them to follow her. She counts out the steps for Nash when he asks her to then she helps him navigate the kitchen by using his clock face example. Their voices float in from the other room and it amazes me how easily she's taken to him.

The other two are still in the living room with me. Trace grunts, "Damn. How did you get a wife like her?"

I chuckle, the words working loose from my brain slowly, "Hell if I know."

# 8
## CADENCE

"SORRY," BRENNON'S SHOULDERS ARE HUNCHED AS HE mutters the word. The guys are leaving, and I've already waved goodbye to all of them. They stayed for the day while the five of us got to know each other. It was the most fun I've had in ages, and I tell Brennon that.

There was something about seeing him interact with his friends. I had a chance to see how much they all care for each other. He's nothing like his cold and cruel family. No, Brennon is warm-hearted and kind. He teased his friends just as much as they teased him, the four of them falling into an easy rhythm.

He starts picking up the house, moving dishes from the table to the sink. Nash made his famous chili for dinner. I didn't know it was possible for a blind man to cook but he just laughed it off, explaining he can do most everything.

It made me wonder about Brennon and the things I may not know about him. Even though I feel awkward, I force myself to say, "Can I ask you some questions? About...about your speaking?"

He looks up from his place by the sink where he's running water for the dishes. He gives me a nod before going back to his task.

I have a million questions to ask, but I start with the first one that comes to my mind. "Were you... always this way?"

He used to be on magazine covers. He was the CEO of his family's company. He had the world at his feet. Then suddenly, it was gone. Just like me, he lost everything. I don't like the realization or the way it makes my chest squeeze tight.

He shakes his head without looking at me.

"So...what happened then?" I don't want to admit that I spent time today searching online and trying to piece together his history. There's no shortage of articles talking of his success, fame, and wealth. Countless interviews show a powerful, articulate man who took his family's already successful company and turned it into an empire. He was cutthroat and ruthless, unstoppable and breath-taking in his power. Then one day, there was an article that he was stepping down to be replaced by his father. In the age of social media with endless ways to gossip, you'd think there would at least be rumors as to what happened. But apparently, the Abernathy family had enough clout to keep every-thing quiet.

He continues washing the dishes for so long that I don't think he's going to answer. I accept his silence and grab a kitchen towel. I dry the dishes alongside him without saying a word.

When we're finally done, he turns to me. There's a faraway look in his eyes. He taps his chest. "Heart." He pauses searching again for the word and finally lets out a frustrated grunt. He reaches for his phone only to push it back on the table.

I'm learning that once he gets frustrated, the words stay inside.

"Maybe we can do charades," I suggest quietly. I don't know if it's the right thing to say. I'm always worried that I'm saying the wrong thing to him. I heard the things his brother said to his face about his ability. I saw the disdain on his parents' faces at the wedding. It makes me sad that they only valued him when he could perform for them, running the family company and creating an undeniable legacy of wealth. I don't want to be like that. I don't want to be another person in a long line that's only cared about him for what he can do.

He taps his chest, the area where his heart is.

I nod. "Heart."

He makes a gesture of a circle.

"Circle. Zero. Number," I call out the words. My father's favorite game is charades. I've lost track of the hours I spent playing it with him growing up. Even now, he loved nothing more than a good game of it at a company party.

Brennon shakes his head and repeats the gesture.

"But it's something round, like a donut."

His face lights up. "Middle."

I think for a second. "The middle of a donut. There's a hole there."

He snaps his fingers as soon as I say the word hole and taps his chest again.

"A hole in your chest?" I shake my head. "A hole in your heart."

Relief flickers across his expression. I don't imagine that the high society people around him ever gave him any patience. He taps the side of his head and manages the word, "Stroke."

"The stroke caused a hole?" I frown.

He makes a gesture for me to reverse the order, and I finally get it. "So, the hole in your heart caused the stroke?" My own heart hurts at the thought. This strong man survived hell, and he did it without the support of anyone. "Are you OK now? Does it still hurt?"

For some crazy reason, I reach out and put my hand on his chest. Even through the thick material of his plaid button down, I feel his steady heartbeat. The sensation sends a wave of relief through me so powerful that I want to drop to my knees in relief.

"OK now," he manages. He takes my hand from his chest and presses a gentle kiss to my palm. With his other hand, he reaches for his buttons, undoing his shirt.

Brennon's chest is broad, just like the rest of him. But it's tanned from hours of work in the sun and covered with a dusting of hair that makes my mouth water. From his strong shoulders down to the happy trail just under his belly button, he's beautifully sculpted everywhere. But I don't think this is the body of a man who works out in a gym for hours each day. No, this is a body earned from working outdoors and caring for his cabin out here alone in the mountains.

He turns slightly and raises his arm. That's when

I spot the small surgical scar along his pec. It's only an inch or two long. He grunts out the word, "Repaired."

"They repaired the hole?" I ask.

When he nods, I take my fingertips and run it over the line. "It took a lot of bravery to survive this."

He shakes his head, something flickering across his face. He doesn't know his own strength. "Ashamed," the word is a soft whisper.

"Why?" My fingertips trail over, circling around his nipple. He shudders at the sensation but doesn't stop me.

He frowns and I can feel the concentration it takes for him to explain to me, "Not...good...man...before."

"You're a good man now," I reassure him. Maybe he was the asshole billionaire everyone accused him of being before. But he's not that man anymore. I know that from the way he defended me in front of Andrew. I know that from the way he fought to become my husband to save me from a terrible marriage. I know that from the way he teased his friends here on the mountain. "Brennon Abernathy is a good man."

I press a kiss against his chest at the same time I flick my finger across his nipple. The resulting growl in the back of his throat has me smiling against his skin. "I'd like to move this conversation to the bedroom."

I don't have to tell Brennon that twice. He scoops me up into his arms and carries me to his bedroom. He sets me on the bed gently, pushing me back. I stare at him and watch the emotions that flicker across his expression. Lust and hunger and something I can't define. Something that could look like affection.

"Just consummation," I remind both of us. It's all this. All it can be. When our marriage is over, I'll make his family pay for what they've done to my father, and he'll hate me then. He'll hate me for destroying the legacy of the company he worked so hard to build.

He doesn't say anything in response as he buries his face in the side of my neck and presses soft kisses to my skin. When we're through, he won't touch me with such tenderness. He won't touch me at all. The thought fills me with pain.

"Kiss me," I whisper, wanting to feel his lips against mine. I want to memorize everything about this moment. About the way he makes love to me so slowly. The way he kisses me gently, the warmth in his eyes, and the way he cups my head like I'm precious to him.

I nudge his shoulder and when he pauses, I roll him onto his back. He's so big and strong, but he goes easily when I push him. He's letting me be in control, and I love it. I press kisses to his chest, where his shirt is still open from my earlier exploration. "You know, there was a really cool scene on page ninety. Something she did to him."

He groans and I lick his nipple. He shudders again, and it makes me feel powerful to know I can make this burly man shiver. When I suck the hard tip into my mouth, he spears his fingers through my hair and groans.

Beneath my body, I feel his hardness surge against my thigh. If it hadn't been for my years of reading smut, I wouldn't even know this was an erogenous zone for a guy. It makes me wonder what else I can do to please Brennon.

After a long moment, I blow on his nipple and turn my attention to the other one. I give it the same attention, delighted when I feel him angle his hips up to grind against my soft body. His hands move to my ass where he kneads and squeezes my cheeks until I'm humping against him. I'm not sure which one of us comes first. I just know that suddenly I'm riding him through our clothes and whispering his name as I come.

Then he's kissing me, stealing all the oxygen from my lungs and I don't mind. I'd give up oxygen forever if it meant I could always feel his tongue against mine. To feel his strong hands roaming along my back and squeezing every inch of my body.

Brennon flips us back over, pinning me beneath his powerful frame. He kisses his way across my body and pulls off my clothes as he goes.

"No fair," I protest when I'm completely naked. "I didn't get to finish what happened on page ninety."

He presses a kiss to my pussy, and I let out a soft sigh. "We'll finish that page later."

He grunts his approval before he ducks his head and licks me. He licks my already soaking body through another release that has me writhing against the sheets and screaming his name.

"Get inside me. Now," I demand when I can finally see again. Despite the earth-shattering orgasms he's given me, I still need him to fill me. I need to feel his big cock stretching me and taking what's his. What's always been his.

He scrambles from the bed and starts yanking on his clothes. He tosses them onto the floor without even looking in their direction and prowls back on the bed.

I spread my thighs wide when I see the big cock that he's wrapped his hand around. He's huge and the thought that it's all for me has anticipation dancing along my skin.

He pauses and looks up at me, his hand still squeezing his weeping shaft. It takes me a second to pull my gaze up. For a moment, I struggle to define the look on my mountain man's face. Shy. He definitely looks shy as he says gently, "Virgin."

I nod, unashamed of my past. I know losing your v-card is a rite of passage to some people, but I never felt the need to get rid of mine just because all of my friends were. No, I wanted to hold out for something special and now that I'm here with Brennon, I'm glad I did. "Yeah, I am one."

The soft smile that lights up his expression makes me feel gooey and warm. "Me…too."

I smile back at him, my body melting into the silk sheets. "That's kind of perfect."

He nods in agreement and kisses me again, long and slow. Our tongues tangle together and it's not until I'm panting again that he pulls away to align our bodies. He thrusts inside slowly, but I'm already so wet that it's not painful like I was expecting. No, the only thing I feel is stuffed full.

He glances at my face, the look on his one of pure awe and wonder. There's a question in his eyes.

"All good," I reassure him with a contented sigh.

He moves in deeper, still giving my body time to get used to his. He continues his steady pace until I wrap a leg around his hips and call his name. His gaze snaps to mine.

"Fuck your wife," I whisper right as I take his earlobe between my teeth and nip at it.

His control snaps and suddenly he's pounding into me and playing with my clit. His grunts fill the air as I chant his name over and over again. Then he's falling over the edge with me, his come shooting into my pussy and spilling all over the sheets.

He lies beside me, his body still intertwined with mine. I face his chest and trace invisible patterns in his skin. I can feel his heart rate slowing down and hear his breathing returning to normal.

He nuzzles my hair and makes soft sounds. I'm not sure what he's saying and I'm too content to figure it out. Instead, I close my eyes and pray this moment can last forever. Because I don't ever want to leave my new husband, not when I've finally found my soulmate.

9

CADENCE

I HUM AS BRENNON COMBS MY WET HAIR IN THE mirror. We're in his bathroom after exploring each other in every possible way. I know how he likes his body touched and the sounds he makes as he comes. I know how he likes to touch me and that he likes my taste.

But for all the things I'm learning about Brennon, he still doesn't know the truth. He doesn't fully understand why we're married. He hasn't once asked me what I'm getting out of it.

"Sad," Brennon growls, touching my face. He places the comb on the counter, still standing behind me. It's a beautiful contrast, this rough mountain man taking such tender care of his new wife.

"It's late. We should go to bed," I tell him, rather than acknowledge that he somehow read my mood. I don't even know where to begin, how to put everything I'm feeling into words.

He shakes his head and is quiet for a moment. His eyebrows crinkle together. They always do that when he's searching for a word. "Tell…me."

I search for my own words. I weigh everything carefully, trying to choose the ones that won't hurt him. The ones that won't make him reject me and hate me forever. "I was marrying Andrew for a business deal."

He growls. He always growls when I say another man's name. I kind of like it, the way he's so possessive. It makes me feel like I'm his and only his.

"I didn't want to. It's complicated." I pick up his comb and run my fingertips along the sharp teeth. Fiddling with it is easier than looking at his expression in the mirror. "My dad spent years tinkering and inventing things. There are patents in his name. Most of it is stuff that will never make it to production. But I never stopped believing in him. Neither did my mom."

My chest feels tight, the way it always does when I think of her. Would she be ashamed of me for what

I've done? She married my father because she was in love with him. Because they were soulmates. I sniff at the thought she'd be disappointed in me for the choices I've made. "She was the prettiest, kindest person you'd ever meet. I lost her when I was just six."

Suddenly, Brennon is in front of me on his knees. He cups my face in his big hand and I can feel the empathy pouring from him. He doesn't say anything. He doesn't have to. The expression on his face tells me that he feels her loss as strongly as I do in this moment.

His features blur as I continue the story, "My dad has never dated since her. He thinks there's an after-life. That Heaven is a real place. He insists she's there waiting for him because she's his soulmate."

Before I met Brennon, I didn't know how he could believe in something so silly. But now that I've found my soulmate, I get it. Because that belief must be the only thing that lets him carry on in the absence of my mother. The only way his heart continues to beat is because he believes he'll see her again.

"He's a good man," I explain. "The best."

My husband wraps his arms around me, pulling me close. I burrow into his chest, not caring that my tears are wetting his skin. I cry for all the things that are wrong. That my mom is gone. That my dad is alone. But most of all, I cry because I've already lost my soulmate.

When I'm able to collect myself, I pull away from his embrace. He grabs a washcloth and cleans my face. I can only imagine what a mess I look like. I want to close my eyes to this. I want to let him carry me back to his bed and touch me until I forget. Instead, I tell him softly, "My dad is in jail now."

Before he can ask me about it, I take a deep breath and say the words that hurt, "And your dad put him there."

---

### Brennon

MY NEW BRIDE LOOKS UP AT ME WITH PUFFY RED EYES, pain etched on her features. "That's why we're married. A marriage into the Abernathy family for my dad's freedom."

I frown, trying to make sense of this. What would my family have to gain from me marrying Cadence? As far as I know, she's not from wealth or fame. She has nothing to offer my parents.

She continues, "I told you my dad is an inventor. One of the designs he created, well, your dad wanted. My dad said no. To get back at him, Jack made it look like my dad is cheating his investors. It's all fake, but nobody will stand up to the Abernathy name."

She smooths down the towel that's wrapped around her luscious body. The towel that I was wrapping around her curvy figure only moments before, feeling like I was on top of the world. Now I'm in the pit of hell. I had no illusions about my marriage. I went in knowing that there was a deal.

But I never expected something like this. It explains why she called me her enemy, why she didn't want to fall in love with me. Too late on my part though. I rub my chest absently, aware of the way it aches so deeply. She'll never want me for real, all because my father is a bastard who takes whatever he wants.

I'll never be able to make her want me or forgive me. But maybe I can find a way to make this right for her. I have to. I can't stand the thought that she's missing her father while he's paying for crimes he never committed.

"I own the majority of my father's company. It was willed to me on my mom's passing. So I went to

Jack and made a deal. My father's technology in exchange for his freedom. Your dad...well, he was the one who added the marriage term."

That sounds just like my father. Of course, he'd find a way to bind her to the family. He's always believed in keeping his enemies close. This is straight out of Jack's playbook. The only question now is how I can fix this for her.

I'm silent for a long time, running the options through my head. There has to be a way to make this better. I'm not stupid enough to believe that she'd stay married to me after I fix this mess. But I can't stand the idea that she's only with me to save her father. That's not love, that's coercion. Fuck my father. Fuck his crooked dealings. Fuck him for taking the only woman I've loved away from me.

"Now you know." She pushes herself off the counter. "I'll grab a sip of water."

I reach for her hand, giving it a gentle squeeze. If there were ever a moment to be miraculously given back my words, this would be it. But they're all lodged in my heart, trapped by the emotions I can't even begin to unpack.

She gives me a sad smile. "It's not your fault."

As soon as she leaves the bathroom, I march into

my bedroom. I search through my stuff until I find my phone. I will fix this, starting tonight.

There are three missed calls from Roman, and a voice message. I listen to him recount the details of Andrew's marriage. It didn't take his hacker long to put the pieces together. But it's the final part that has my heart sinking, "Her dad was transferred to the hospital today. Suspected pneumonia. He's in rough shape. They've been trying to get in touch with her. I sent you a text with the hospital address."

As soon as the message finishes, I take my phone to Cadence and play it for her. Her face pales. For a moment, I think she's going to cry again. "He's my whole world."

I touch her shoulder. Before our marriage, I never would have understood what she just said. But now I do. Because this beautiful woman in front of me is my whole world.

She stands there unmoving, and I realize she must be in shock. I lead her to the bedroom and help her into a pair of yoga pants and one of her t-shirts. I pull her hair back into a ponytail and help her into shoes. The entire time, I'm doing my best to reassure her. It's all coming out as a jumble of words, but she seems to calm at the rumble of my voice.

The trip down the mountain takes longer than

normal because I'm driving through the snowy roads in the dark. I won't risk an accident with her beside me, so I send up a prayer that her father lives. That she gets to see him again. That by some miracle, I can untangle all of this.

When we arrive at the hospital, we're directed down a hall to the room where her father is being kept.

The guard outside stops me because I'm not considered immediate family. I growl at him, prepared to take him down. There's nothing that will keep me from supporting my girl right now when she needs it.

But Cadence puts a hand on my chest. Her touch instantly settles me, and I flick my gaze to hers.

She gives me a sad smile. "It's probably best if he doesn't see an Abernathy. You should...you should go."

The words are like a dagger to my chest. I want to be here. I want to support her. I want her to know that she never faces anything alone again.

She continues, oblivious to the way she twists the dagger. "This was a mistake. We should see about a quickie divorce." She lifts her chin, ever the defiant queen. "Thanks for what you've done. I'll find a way to help my father from here."

Then she leans up on her tip toes and presses a soft kiss to my cheek. She disappears into her father's hospital room while I'm left staring after her. I don't know what the hell gave her the impression that we were a mistake, but it's one more thing I plan to correct.

# 10

# CADENCE

I'M STARING AT A GHOST. HE USED TO BE TEN FEET tall with a head full of gray hair and the imposing stare of a man half his age. But here under the hospital lights in the jail uniform, my dad looks sallow.

His breathing is slow and measured, every breath a struggle even with the oxygen tube attached to his nose. But it's the metal cuffs around his wrists that have me pressing a hand to my mouth. I hate the way he's chained to the bed like an animal. I can't even give him a hug.

The officer in the corner barely acknowledges my presence. He's clearly decided I'm not a threat, so he continues sipping his paper cup of coffee and staring at the TV with the constant stream of news chatter.

Dad blinks open his eyes, they're glassy from being sick. His gaze rakes down me, searching for the cause of my distress. "You look like shit."

I force myself to offer him a smile that I don't feel. My heart splintered into a million pieces before I set foot in this room. I called everything with Brennon a mistake.

"You don't look so hot yourself," I counter. He hasn't let me visit him since he was arrested eight weeks ago. I understand that he didn't want me to see him in his inmate uniform, but it still hurt. It hurts even worse to know he's been so sick.

"Just a touch of cold," he mutters before breaking into a coughing fit. I grab the nearby pink pitcher and pour him water. I help him sip from the cup before he says, "It takes more than this to keep your old man down."

"I know," I whisper, my eyes filling with tears.

"Don't do this, sweet pea. Tell me something good, something that makes you smile," Dad says. It's what he always said to me when I was a kid, and I was having a bad day. It usually helped to turn things around. But I'm not a kid anymore and life isn't that simple. Now, it's complicated. Really complicated thanks to a certain mountain man.

"They finally opened up that sushi restaurant near my apartment," I tell him. It opened a few days ago. I wasn't there for the grand opening since I was busy getting married, but he doesn't need to know that part.

I move to the purple recliner next to his bed. I keep my movements slow in case that officer nearby suddenly decides to take an interest in me. But he's still focused on the TV. I sit, my muscles aching from all the things I did together with Brennon. I can't think about him right now, so instead I tell my dad, "I'll take you there when we get out."

I pass the next hour by making promises to my father. All the things we'll do and the places we'll go. The adventures we'll have. By the time, he finally drifts into a light slumber, he has a smile on his face.

My phone dings from my purse, but I quickly turn it off. I don't want to talk to anyone right now. I just want to wake up from this terrible nightmare. I want to go back to that shitty apartment when I was a waitress, and my dad was a janitor. Back then, I found twenty dollars at the laundromat and bought us all the seafood we could eat from that little restaurant down at the pier. Life was simpler back then.

Visiting hours are officially over, but the officer across the room is snoring loudly. Over the course of my conversation with my dad, I learned the man's name is Oliver. Apparently, he and my dad are friends. Well, I guess as much friends as two people can be in this situation.

I lean back in my chair keeping watch over my father until my eyes are dry and gritty. How many nights did he do this when we were homeless? How many times did he stay awake, silently standing guard so I would be safe through the night?

The sun is just starting to lighten the sky with shades of pink and orange when a nurse comes bustling into the room to take my father's vitals. She does her job, quickly and efficiently. She leaves with promises the doctor will be in soon just as the breakfast tray arrives.

He waves away the food and asks the officer to turn up the news channel. His favorite segment, the one on local businesses, will be on soon. My dad might love inventing new things, but he's also fascinated by business topics. He's a hell of an entrepreneur. He always has been. When this is done, I'm going to help him rebuild. I don't know how, but I'll figure it out.

While he's busy with that, a second officer comes into the room. He has a hushed conversation with Oliver, and I assume they're changing shifts. But then Oliver approaches the bed and reaches for the cuffs. He unlocks them, careful not to hurt my father. "Walt, they're saying charges against you are being dropped."

"What?" My father and I both stare at Oliver, trying to compute this information.

"As of six this morning, you're a free man," Oliver claps him gently on the shoulder with a smile. "I don't know who you know, but somebody has pull. I heard the governor called the warden on his personal line in the middle of the night."

I gasp. There's only one family with that much power. Did Jack finally make good on his word? Did he release my father without knowing what I said to Brennon about the divorce?

Dad's gaze moves to me. "Who?"

"The Abernathy family has that kind of power," I say rather than explain to my dad that I've been making deals with them. It's going to break his heart when he finds out. But this can't stay a secret for much longer, especially when Brennon appears on the TV screen.

He's standing on a platform, looking out at a room filled with journalists and other media professionals. He's wearing his usual outfit, a plaid button down and blue jeans. His beard is neat, and his hair is pulled into a ponytail. He doesn't look a thing like the CEO that once took the tech industry by storm. No, he looks like a gruff mountain man. My gruff mountain man.

I blink and rub my tired eyes. I have to be imagining this. Brennon hasn't been in the public eye since his stroke. His family has gone to great lengths to hide him away and now here he is, letting the world see his face.

His friend Trace adjusts the microphone for him while Nash and Roman stand off to the side. They look like they're ready to go to battle for him. They have his back and that means the world to me.

Dad is still asking me questions, but I'm too curious to answer them. Instead, I focus all my attention on Brennon. A hushed silence falls over the crowd as they eagerly wait for word from the former leader.

He stares down at cue cards that he was tapping against his palm only a few seconds ago. I can feel his frustration mount, the things he wants to say all building up inside of him. More than anything, I wish I could go to him and put a hand on his arm. I wish I could remind him that he's so much more than they see. Brennon Abernathy is a good man.

Finally, he looks up from the cards and says in a halting tone, "Two years...I had...stroke."

A flurry of questions starts from the crowd, but he holds up his hand. A king silencing his subjects. The crowd quiets, and he continues, "Since then...I have....reflected. Company has...done...wrong. Family wrong."

He scrubs a hand through his face, looking for the words. I can't imagine what this is costing him to be up there. His pride and dignity. The man he used to be was refined and polished. He never stumbled when he spoke and kept a perfect rich baritone with every word.

But this man struggles for each syllable and when he speaks into the microphone, it's a deep rumble. His voice is more growl than anything from the months without use. "Worst wrong...is... prism...prism..."

Trace puts a hand on his shoulder and leans close to say something in his ear. But Brennon shakes his head and forces himself to continue, "Wrongful… imprisonment. Walter…Beauford."

"What is the boy doing?" Dad frowns. "He didn't know nothing. This was Jack's fault!"

I shush him, my attention still glued to the screen.

He looks to Trace who nods that he got the words out correctly. Meanwhile the crowd has erupted into a new round of questions that's nearly deafening.

He waits again until they're quiet. The concentration etched on his face tells me he isn't done with his message. "Walt, I…am…sorry."

With that, he turns to Trace. His friend claps him on the back. I'm pretty sure he tells him he did good before he leans forward to the microphone, "Follow up questions can be directed to me, Trace."

My heart skips a beat. "He did this for me. I know he did."

Dad reaches for the remote, silencing the TV. In the middle of the conference, the two officers left the room, and I didn't even notice. I was too busy paying attention to Brennon and his stuttered confession. He was so brave and all I want to do is go to him.

"What do you mean he did it for you?"

I sniff and swipe at my face before I explain to my dad what happened over the past few weeks. I don't leave any of the details out. I tell him about going to Jack to plead for mercy, about agreeing to marry Andrew, and how Brennon stepped in at the last minute. I tell him everything except about those private moments in Brennon's bedroom. "You were right, Dad. He didn't know anything about what was going on with you."

My dad takes my hand and gives it a gentle squeeze. "And now you love him."

It's not a question, but I still nod. I'm caught in an impossible situation. I can't betray either of them. "He's my soulmate."

"Then go to him," Dad answers.

It's not that simple. There's so much to untangle, so many messy things about this situation. Even if he did get all charges against my father dropped, there's still the shit storm he unleashed on his own father. "He—his family—"

Dad waves a hand. "I know my daughter. She has a good heart, and if she loves this man, there is something good in him. Now, go on. Get out of here. Don't you know sick old men need to rest? Oliver!"

When the officer pokes his head in the room, Dad takes another wheezing breath before he says,

"My girl needs an escort to the Asheville coliseum where that press conference is happening. Think you can get her there before her fellow leaves?"

Oliver grins. "Let's do it."

I press a kiss to Dad's cheek and promise to come back later. He grunts at me. "Don't you waste your energy on me. You spend time with your boy."

I hope I can get there in time to tell Brennon how I feel, how much his speech meant to me, and how desperately I hope that the two of us can stay married.

# 11

# BRENNON

As Trace answers the last question, I'm struck with an overwhelming wave of exhaustion. My friends and I have been up all night, uncovering every dirty deed that Jackson Abernathy has committed and there have been many. The worst part is the same crimes that he accused Walter of, he's done himself.

I knew better than to go to the local police. My father already owns them, so while the conference was taking place, Roman's hacker friend was releasing the files online. Every time it was taken down from one site, it was uploaded to three new ones. It's spreading across the internet like wildfire and already sparking public outrage.

The price of company stock is plummeting and

within a few hours, there will only be steaming wreckage.

I conclude the conference, and the four of us make our way to the suite reserved for performers and politicians who take the coliseum stage. Once, I would have felt at home on the expensive couch with the thousand-dollar bottles of wine in the bar area. Now nothing feels like home without Cadence. She's why I did this. I wouldn't blame her if she never wants to see my face again. Not after the things I discovered about my family. But I have to find a way to win her over, and it starts with this.

"You did good today," Nash says as he takes the seat on the sofa across from me.

I nod, accepting the praise even though it was a team effort. Without Nash, Trace, and Roman, none of this would have been possible.

"They have your dad in custody already. Your mom turned herself in as of three minutes ago," Roman confirms.

"Drew?" I grind out the word. He was part of a hit-and-run a year ago. He was driving drunk when he hit an elderly lady and left her in a snow drift to die. She survived, but the police never could find any suspects. Of course, my father had records. He kept careful records of every time he helped that shit stain escape the consequences of his actions. Those went public too.

"They have eyes on Andrew. He's booked a flight overseas. As soon as he arrives at the airport, they'll get him," Roman answers.

I nod, my mind at ease knowing that the last piece of the puzzle is falling into place. As soon as I saw the reports, the elderly woman and her family suddenly had a generous benefactor who paid off her medical bills and her home. There are scholar-ships for her grandchildren now and her retirement fund is flush. She'll never want for anything again. It's far from what she deserves. No one should suffer the way she did, but maybe today is a tiny step toward justice for her.

"Our guys are ten minutes out," Trace tells me. He and Roman hired a crew of bodyguards to get us out of here. This little press conference cost me my anonymity. Reporters and journalists are going to be crawling all over my life for the next few months. For two years, there has been speculation about what happened to Brennon Abernathy, and now the world finally knows. The shit storm is only beginning.

Nash passes me a chilled water. "You heard from her yet?"

I shake my head. I don't expect to. I need to woo my girl. It's going to take a hell of a lot more than one damn press conference to convince her that we can be together.

There's a knock on the door and Roman moves to open it. He ushers our guests on through, a cop and…Cadence. She's actually standing here in front of me. Twisting her fingers together and biting her lip. She looks like she hasn't slept since last night. Her yoga pants and t-shirt are rumpled. Her ponytail is messy, and her face is tear-streaked.

"Out," I growl to my friends. They don't get to see her like this, looking vulnerable and miserable. Nobody does because I'm her shield, the man who stands in front of her no matter what life throws our way.

No one has to be told twice. They all scurry from the room, and I slam the door closed after them. I lock it so we won't be disturbed. Then I pick her up in my arms and settle with her on the couch. She's in my lap but she makes no effort to move. I'm counting that as a win today.

I put my finger under her chin, tilting her face toward me. "How…father?" I manage to get enough of the sentence out, worried that her tears have to do with her father. I haven't gotten a report that her father's condition has worsened. But right now, I'm getting thrown so much information that it's possible I missed the message.

"He's going to be OK," she says and lets out a sigh. The one motion has all the energy draining from her body and she settles against my chest. My hand instantly goes to her back, and I rub slow, soothing circles. I know what she said last night, but I also know she didn't mean it. She couldn't have. We're meant to be.

"I…" She drops her gaze from my face to my shirt collar. "Thank you for what you did. Up there."

I want her to know exactly why I did that. "I… love…you."

Just like that, the words are out there. But they don't feel as scary as I always imagined they would. Maybe because I know even if she won't say them back, she feels them too.

She presses her forehead to mine. "I love you too, my big mountain man."

"No divorce," I growl at her. I'm never letting this woman go, no matter what I have to say or do, she'll always be mine. I'll follow her to the ends of the earth and give away my entire fortune. I'll move to damn California and become a hippie if that's what it takes. But I'll never, ever let this woman out of my sight again.

She lets out a shaky chuckle, her breath warm against my skin. "No divorce."

I take her mouth in a kiss, deepening it when she whimpers. She shifts on my lap, spreading her thighs around me. Fuck, I love this. I love the way she's grinding against me and panting into my mouth.

I reach for her shirt, shrugging out of it. She's not wearing a bra, her tits swinging free. I wrap my lips around a pink bud and suck it into my mouth. She tastes like heaven everywhere, and I'll never get enough of this. I'll never get enough of pleasing my beautiful wife.

She groans softly and arches against me, letting me have my way with her bountiful breasts. She tugs on my ponytail to get my attention, calling my name in that breathy tone of hers.

Reluctantly, I release her nipple. It's hard to focus through the haze of need and lust that's coursing through my body. All this woman has to do is look at me and I'm hard as steel. I don't ever see that changing, even after we've been together for decades.

"I want to live with you," She says then adds the next word softly as if she's feeling shy, "Forever."

"Forever," I repeat around the lump in my

throat. I've found my forever. I thought I'd always be alone in my mountain cabin but thanks to this woman, the place is a home now. I can't wait until we can fill it with children. I want a dozen daughters that look like their mama. I want to spoil them day and night.

Just the thought of her belly round with my kid ignites a new wave of lust and suddenly, I can't get this woman's clothes off fast enough. I reach for the center of her pants. They're already wet and the thin material gives way easy enough.

She lets out a little gasp, but I don't give her time to even process what I'm doing before I've shoved her underwear to the side and sunk my fingers knuckle-deep into her wet pussy. My thumb finds her clit and I strum it lightly.

She rides my hand like the good girl she is, always so responsive to my touch. She's panting as she comes, desperate for the release that only I can give her. When I kiss her neck and suck on her soft skin, she detonates.

It's so fuckin' beautiful to watch the ecstasy on my woman's face, to know I'm the one that gave her body these shudders of pleasure. It makes me feel like a king, a king who's found his queen.

As her channel slowly relaxes again, I pull my

cock from my pants and slide into her wet heat. We both groan at the contact, at the way it feels so right.

"Mine," I whisper into her ear before I take her lobe, nipping at it.

Cadence spasms around me, just the way I knew she would. Then she flicks my nipple causing me to thrust deeper into her. "And you're mine."

We come together, a sweaty mess. But I don't care. Everything is right now that my girl is in my arms again with my come dripping between her legs. I'll keep her nice and full of it until I get that first baby pumped into her.

She snuggles into my chest and lets out a contented sigh. "I'm really glad you came to your brother's wedding."

I chuckle and press a kiss to her hair. She's not the only one. I'll always be glad that I punched my brother in the face and took his bride for my own. Because Cadence? She belongs to me and only me. She will for the rest of her life.

12

CADENCE

"Are you sure about this?" Dad asks Brennon again.

Brennon holds open his truck door. It's the early morning hours at the hospital and dad has just been released after a three week stay. He was driving the nurse crazy by week two. He was healthy enough to be discharged then, but Brennon pulled some strings to keep him in there longer. That's because our lives are a media circus right now.

I can't even buy lemons at the grocery store without a reporter sticking a camera in my face and asking me how I feel about the Abernathy family. That didn't go over very well with Brennon. He ruined the man's camera and threatened him if he ever came near me again. Yeah, my burly mountain man makes for an excellent bodyguard.

After the press conference, it made national headlines when it was discovered that Brennon and I are married. We're apparently considered the Romeo and Juliet of Asheville, which just makes me roll my eyes. Our story has a much better ending.

Brennon reaches for my dad and helps him into the truck with ease. My dad is still weak from the pneumonia and the doctor estimates it may take him another week or two before he finally beats it. He has a nebulizer, and I've been given strict instructions on symptoms to watch for. But I don't expect to see any of those. He's out of the woods and at this point, it's all just a waiting game.

Once he's in the car, Brennon helps me into the passenger seat, pausing to press a kiss to my forehead. He's so affectionate, no matter who we're in front of. I love the way he's never ashamed to show his love for me.

I look up in time to see my father beaming in the backseat. As soon as Brennon and I left the coliseum that day, he insisted on coming to the hospital to meet my father. With tears in his eyes, he apologized in his halting speech.

My dad just threw his arms around Brennon and asked, "How can I hate my new son?"

Just like that, everything was fine between them. They actually share a few hobbies and when Dad is well again, they plan on going fishing together.

Brennon's family is in jail. He's not upset about it, but sometimes, it makes me sad for him. I want him to have a big, loving family. Although with how often Brennon and I make love, it wouldn't surprise me if we build that big, loving family pretty fast.

As Brennon starts the drive back to his cabin—well, our cabin now—he threads his fingers through mine. Just his touch is enough to have me squeezing my thighs together. I don't think I'll ever get enough of this gruff man or the way he loves me so completely.

When we arrive at the cabin, Brennon's friends are already inside. Nash brought a cake and there are decorations and party hats. I smile at what they've done. While he was in the hospital, they adopted my dad. The three of them visited him daily, sneaking him treats and playing card games with him. After eight weeks of being isolated from everyone he knew, it was good for my dad to be welcomed back to society so warmly.

He grins at the celebration and enjoys talking

with the guys. But eventually, I can tell he's getting tired. His energy levels still aren't quite where they should be. The doctor said to expect him to be tired and need extra rest for the following month.

Nash seems to be the first to notice his exhaustion. He stretches his own neck and says, "It's getting late. I have to get home. Something ain't quite right there."

"What's wrong with your place?" Dad asks as he pushes away his plate of celebratory cake.

Nash shrugs, his head turned in my father's direction. "Seems like someone is watching my place. Staking it out or something."

Trace snorts. "At least, it's better than Roman. He knows who's coming and going at his place. Just won't do nothing about it."

Roman shoots him a look that I can't decipher. Sometimes, these guys have so many of their own inside jokes and quips, it's like listening to another language.

"We'll be on our way then," Trace says, seeming to realize his misstep.

Nash stands and after a flurry of goodbyes, the three of them are gone. I help my father to his room while Brennon gathers the dishes. He's promised to make steak later for my dad when he wakes up from his nap.

"You seem happy here," Dad remarks as he kicks off his shoes in the guest bedroom. Brennon has made it clear that he's welcome to stay as long as he wants.

"I am happy," I quickly reassure him. "I'm the happiest I've ever been. I only wish Mom were here."

He gives my hand a squeeze. "She is. Any time you're happy, she's smiling down on you."

"Then she's always with me," I answer, thinking of how happy I am all the time. I press a kiss to his cheek. "You sleep now, and when you wake up, we'll make you dinner. All your favorites."

"A man could get used to being waited on like this," he chuckles as he settles on the bed, reaching for the quilt at the bottom.

"Well, get used to it because it's happening every day," I promise. I stay with him until his breathing goes shallow and his body relaxes. Then I slip from the room to find my husband.

He's in the office, exactly where I expected him to be. The Abernathy company is nothing but rubble. It's been picked clean by greedy companies that were eager to buy up the talent and the tech behind it.

But after talking about it, my dad and I asked Brennon to become the head of our company. He's inheriting a mess, but if there's any man up to the task, we know it's him. He'll do right by my father and the company. Most importantly, he'll do right by his wife.

It's not Brennon's dream to run another company. He's happy here in his cabin, building things and reading his books. But he promised to get the company in great shape before passing it off to the next CEO.

Brennon has already started building a workshop on the property. It's for my father, but I suspect the two of them will spend most of their time out there together.

He peers at the computer screen, his gaze flicking between the spreadsheet on it and the spreadsheet up on his laptop. His plaid button-down is rolled up, revealing his thick, hairy forearms. I love the way his brows are crinkled in concentration and how he strokes his thick beard as he puzzles through the numbers.

I knock on the door to get his attention and grin when he looks up at me. "Excuse me, Mr. Abernathy, I have those reports you were looking for."

He laughs then, a rich sound. After everything

we've been through, I'm glad we can both laugh and play together. Because I definitely like playing with my mountain man.

He rounds the desk and picks me up. I've learned that he loves carrying me. It doesn't matter if it's just across the cabin, he's always looking for an excuse to pull me close to his chest. Not that I can complain. I feel safest and happiest when I'm in my husband's arms.

He settles me on the desk and instantly steps between my parted knees. I reach out and put a hand to his chest. There's something I wanted to talk to him about and if he starts kissing me, we definitely won't get any talking done. "I've been thinking. Well, thinking and talking with my dad. He was on board with this too."

Brennon nods, focusing on my lips as I talk. He likes to do that a lot.

I fight a hot blush all over. I know what that look means, and I know the way it ends. Usually with me under my man, begging for his cock before screaming his name in ecstasy. "This is serious."

He makes the gesture for an invisible halo above his head.

I roll my eyes. My husband is the dirtiest of sinners when he gets me alone, and I love every minute of it. "I want to take over the company. When you've set it to rights. We'd both like it to stay in the family."

He tips my face up. "I...believe...in...you."

"Does that mean you'll be my mentor? It would mean lots of one-on-one sessions." I reach for the waistband of his jeans, pulling out his already hard shaft. I stroke my fingers up and down it. "I'll need lots of hands-on training."

He groans, thrusting his hips forward.

"I'm taking that as a yes," I tease.

I shouldn't have teased him because the moment the words leave my lips, Brennon flips me around. He pulls up my skirt and yanks on my underwear until they rip. I've given up trying to get him to be gentle on my panties. He's told me before he hates anything that keeps him from his pussy, so now I just figure extra panties into the budget every month.

The budget is the last thing I'm thinking about as I brace myself against the wood. He enters me in one smooth stroke, and I sigh. When my man is pumping into me, everything feels right in my world.

His breath is hot against my ear as he reaches around to play with my clit. He's murmuring sweet nothings under his breath as he touches me. I'm not sure what he's saying because the words and the sensations all blur together until I'm coming on his cock, just the way he likes.

His release starts seconds after mine and he holds me through it, pressing soft kisses to my shoulder. When it's over, we hold each other in his chair. He makes me feel so loved and precious. "I can't wait until we have babies to spoil together."

"Soon," he growls in my ear, and I feel him starting to get hard all over again. If there's one thing that turns my man on, it's talking about getting pregnant.

I laugh. "At this rate, definitely soon."

I smile at the thought. I'm looking forward to having a family with my mountain man. He's given me everything, and I can't wait to give him beautiful babies for us to cuddle together.

# EPILOGUE

## BRENNON

"Do you think he'll be lonely?" My wife chews on her bottom lip as she gazes at our cabin. We've never left him alone for the past six months. Part of that is because my wife hovers over him.

I take her hand in mine and press a soft kiss to her knuckles, silently reassuring her that her dad is fine. He's made a complete recovery from the pneumonia and is in better health than most men half his age.

All of the charges against him were dropped and he's now free to spend his time tinkering. I built him a workshop on the edge of the property and that's where he goes most days. I join him there in the afternoons.

In the mornings, I'm all Cadence's. We spend that

time making love on every available surface in the office and sometimes, we even get a little bit of work done.

She's taken over running her father's company and she's doing an amazing job at it. She still asks me a lot of questions. She's more than capable of doing everything on her own, and I've reassured her of that countless times. But she likes including me in the business decisions, so I weigh in when she asks. The rest of the time, I'm her silent partner, supporting her from the sidelines.

"You're right." She gives me a soft smile. "He'll be fine. Of course, he'll be fine. Your friends will be checking in on him, and I'm sure Nash will bring him some of his homemade cake."

My friends continue to be her dad's biggest supporters. In fact, he's a regular fixture at all of our poker nights and BBQs. I think Roman may have even talked him into joining us on our next hike. I don't mind having my father-in-law around. He's a good guy. The kind of man that knows what it's like to go through the fire and come out on the other side with deep scars.

I put my arm around my wife's shoulders, pulling her to me. She scoots across the bench seat coming into my embrace willingly. I press soft kisses to her forehead, her eyelids, her cheeks. Anywhere I can put my lips, I want to.

She melts into the seat, relaxing under my lips. She always does. "Sorry. We don't have to talk about him. This is our honeymoon."

We've been married just over six months, and I finally convinced her to let me take her on a honeymoon. It's not that she didn't want to go on a honeymoon. She's just been adjusting to her new role as CEO and nursing her father back to health. My woman is a rockstar, and it's time I took a week to take care of her and remind her just how incredible she is.

She lets out a little sigh. "Mmm, you better start the truck soon or we're going to start the honeymoon early."

I chuckle. She's been a horny thing lately. She's always reaching for me, and I'm always reaching for her. But the past month, it's been different. We can't keep our hands off each other. We're going at it two and three times a day. We must really be in the honeymoon stage.

Finally, I pull away from her long enough to start the truck. When I asked where she wanted to go, she told me she wanted to see Rainbow Falls. I offered the world, any extraordinary destination she could think of. Surfing in Kuta. Shopping in Paris. Skydiving in Costa Rica.

But my woman wanted to see the natural waterfall in our own backyard. I booked us the honeymoon suite at a local bed and breakfast. The place was described online as quaint and charming. I know it'll delight Cadence to see it and walk the streets of the nearby town of Brevard. If we're lucky, we might even get to see one of the white squirrels the area is known for.

She chatters for the first few minutes of the drive, telling me things about her childhood and the way she hopes to raise our children. We don't have any yet, and I thought maybe something was wrong. But Cash, the town doctor, reassured me that it can take up to a year of trying to conceive before it actually happens. I'm trying to be patient, but I can't wait to see my woman pregnant with my baby.

Walt is up for it, too. He's been dropping hints about how nice it'd be to have some grandkids for the past two months. I don't think it's a coincidence that he's started to work on creating kids' toys. He's just as eager as we are to see the next generation of the Abernathy family start.

All of my family members are in jail. Mom pleaded guilty and agreed to testify against my father for the part she's played in the company's shady dealings. She's already a few months into a ten-year sentence. But my dad is dragging his case on and on. His lawyers keep asking for continuances and pulling these bogus "motions" in an attempt to delay his trial. At least, he's on house arrest so he can't flee the country.

Andrew did manage to flee the authorities, but my idiot brother picked a country that has an extradition treaty with ours. He's now back at home and awaiting trial for what he did, among several other crimes. I suspect he'll plea out before he can face sentencing.

For all of this, I wanted to change my name. Abernathy felt like a shameful legacy, but my beautiful wife changed my mind.

She scowled at me when I suggested it and insisted that she is an Abernathy too. "Are you ashamed of me as well? What about the children we'll have one day? The legacy of your name is what you make it, and I happen to be very proud of the Abernathy name. To me, it represents a man who is honest and good and true. Who takes responsibility for his wrongs and always tries to make the world a better place. I can't think of a legacy I'd want to give my children more."

When she said that, I couldn't help but feel like the luckiest man in the world. Not only does my wife love me, I have her unconditional support. I'll never take that for granted, and I'll always support her dreams.

After a few minutes, she stops talking and drifts to sleep. Her head is on my shoulder and the feeling of her so close never fails to warm me. But she's been sleeping a lot lately. When we come back into town, I'll set up a doctor's appointment for her. I want her to see Dr. Cash and have her vitamin levels checked. If her vitamins are normal, I'll insist she hire an assistant to lighten her workload.

We finally arrive at the little bed and breakfast. She's looking paler than normal and she touches her stomach. "Ugh, I don't think I should have eaten that burrito dad made for breakfast."

Her father loves cooking and the two of us often trade-off. I quickly learned my wife doesn't enjoy being in the kitchen—unless I'm taking her up against one of the counters. Then she doesn't mind it so much.

I pat my own stomach. Breakfast is sitting right with me. Of course, a lot of things aren't sitting right with her. Trace came into the cabin the other day with cigar smoke on his clothes, and she couldn't be

in the same room with him. Yeah, she's definitely
going to the doctor when we get back.

She tries to reach for the suitcases, but I scowl
down at her and take them. Check-in is a smooth
process but she's looking sicker and sicker. By the
time we get to the suite, she dashes for the
bathroom.

I hold her hair back while she empties her stomach. When she's done, she swirls mouthwash and I
go for my phone. I've already started to dial Cash's
number when she frowns at me. "What are you
doing?"

"Doc," I manage the word.

"I don't need a doctor," she insists.

I quirk an eyebrow. This is one fight she's not
winning. She isn't well and if that means we have to
cancel the honeymoon and go back to town so she
can receive proper care, then that's what we'll do.
"Sick."

"I'm not…" She presses a hand to her forehead.
"I'm not sick."

I punch in the last digits and she reaches for the
phone, quickly wrestling it from my grip. She glares
up at me. "I think I'm pregnant, you big doofus."

The floor tilts at the single word. *Pregnant.*

Could it be that all of our dreams are about to

come true? Did we really make a little life? A piece of me and a piece of her came together, just like that?

She gestures with her hand. "I realized last night that I've missed a couple of periods, but the store wasn't open. Besides, I didn't want you to find out that way. I meant to grab one from the gas station. But I fell asleep."

Pregnancy test. She needs to take a pregnancy test. I turn toward the bathroom door, a man on a mission.

"Where are you going?" She calls after me.

"Test," I growl out the word and stalk toward the door. I don't know why I'm bothering to do this. I already feel it deep in my gut. All the pieces of the past few days are sliding into place. How horny she is. How tired she is. The weird cravings and sudden aversions to certain scents.

Twenty minutes later, I'm back with ten different pregnancy test brands. I didn't know which one was right, so I just grabbed a bunch of them. I also grabbed chocolate and a teddy bear. It's the sort of stuff I'd normally grab when I'm making a tampon run so it seemed like the right thing to do.

She takes the test then the two of us wait. We're staring down at a little white stick, silently willing it to tell us the most important news of our lives.

"It'll be OK if I'm not…right?" She sniffs. Fuck, sometimes I forget how much she wants a baby too. How she looks at the women in town with babies and toddlers and the sheer longing that crosses her face. If I could, I would have given her a baby months ago.

I cup her face and stare deep into her eyes. "I… love you…no…matter…what."

Whether we have no kids or a dozen, we're already a family in my eyes. Adding a kid would just be a way of making it bigger.

My timer dings, and she closes her eyes. "Just tell me."

I glance at the little stick and for a second, I can't breathe. That pink line. The instructions said that line means she's pregnant. Gratitude for this gift and awe for my incredible woman slam into me at the same time. I put my hand on her stomach and give her a nod, my own gaze filling with tears.

She squeals and throws her arms around me. "I'm so happy! I was starting to worry it wouldn't happen for us."

I pepper her face and neck and hair with kisses. Anywhere I can get my lips, I'm putting them on her. We did this. We made a little life.

Gently, I lift her up and carry her to the hotel

suite bed where I spend the rest of the day making love to my wife and the mother of my child. She's my best friend, my soulmate, and I plan to show her that every day for the rest of our lives.

---

**Want a bonus scene with Brennon and Cadence? Sign up for my weekly newsletter and get the bonus here.**

## READ NEXT: OWNED BY THE MOUNTAIN MAN

*Can this curvy thief steal the grumpy mountain man's heart after a break-in gone wrong?*

**Laura**

I wasn't breaking and entering. I was on my way to grandma's house. That's the honest truth. The fact that I'm dressed like a cat burglar should be of no importance to anyone. Not even the hot mountain man whose cabin I accidentally stumbled into.

The coming snowstorm is unexpected...so is the citizen's arrest. The problem is I've never wanted to let anyone search me so badly. This mountain man might be gruff and grumpy, but he's welcome to handcuff me anytime.

**Nash**

Yeah, she was on her way to grandma's house. And I'm the big, bad wolf. Although I can't deny that there's definitely something in me that wants to eat her up, this snowstorm is the only thing keeping her here.

As soon as I can, I'm washing my hands of trouble and turning her over to the sheriff. That was my plan. But the more time I spend around the curvy little thief, the more I think it's my heart that's in danger.

If you love a grumpy alpha male who falls hard and loves his curvy woman fiercely, it's time to meet Nash in Owned by the Mountain Man.

Read Laura and Nash's Story

COURAGE COUNTY SERIES

Welcome to Courage County where protective alpha heroes fall for strong curvy women they love and defend. There's NO cheating and NO cliffhangers. Just a sweet, sexy HEA in each book.

**Love on the Ranch**

Her Alpha Cowboy

Pregnant and alone, Riley has nowhere to go until the alpha cowboy finds her. Will she fall in love with her rescuer?

Her Older Cowboy

Summer is making a baby with her brother's best friend. But he insists on making it the old-fashioned way.

Her Protector Cowboy

Jack will do whatever it takes to protect his curvy woman after their hot one-night stand…then he plans to claim her!

Her Forever Cowboy

Dean is in love with his best friend's widow. When they're stranded together for the night, will he finally tell her how he feels?

Her Dirty Cowboy

The ranch's newest hire also happens to be the woman Adam had a one-night stand with…and she's carrying his baby!

Her Sexy Cowboy

She's a scared runaway with a baby. He's determined to protect them both. But neither of them expected to fall in love.

Her Wild Cowboy

He'll keep his curvy woman safe, even if it means a marriage in name only. But what happens when he wants to make it a real marriage?

Her Wicked Cowboy

One hot night with Jake gave me the best gift of my life: a beautiful baby girl. Will he want us to be a family when I show up on his doorstep a year later?

**Courage County Brides**

The Cowboy's Bride

The only way out of my horrible life is to become a mail order bride. But will my new cowboy husband be willing to take a chance on love?

The Cowboy's Soulmate

Can a jaded playboy find forever with his curvy mail order bride and her baby? Or will her secret ruin their future?

The Cowboy's Valentine

I'm a grumpy loner cowboy and I like it that way. Until my beautiful mail order bride arrives and suddenly, I want more than a marriage in name only.

The Cowboy's Match

Will this mail order bride matchmaker take a chance on love when she falls for the bearded cowboy who happens to be her VIP client?

The Cowboy's Obsession

Can this stalker cowboy show the curvy schoolteacher that he's the one for her?

The Cowboy's Sweetheart

Rule #1 of becoming a mail order bride: never fall in love with your cowboy groom.

The Cowboy's Angel

Can this cowboy single dad with a baby find love with his new mail order bride?

The Cowboy's Heiress

This innocent heiress is posing as a mail order bride. But what happens when her grumpy cowboy husband discovers who she really is?

## Courage County Warriors

Rescue Me

Getting out was hard. Knowing who to trust was easy: my dad's best friend. He's the only man I can count on, but will we be able to keep our hands off each other?

Protect Me

When I need a warrior to protect me, I know just who to turn to: my brother's best friend. But will this grumpy cowboy who's guarding my body break my heart?

Shield Me

When trouble comes for me, I know who to call—my ex-boyfriend's dad. He's the only one who can help. But can I convince this grumpy cowboy to finally claim me?

### Courage County Fire & Rescue

The Firefighter's Curvy Nanny

As a single dad firefighter, I was only looking for a quick fling. Then the curvy woman from last night shows up. Turns out, she's my new nanny.

The Firefighter's Secret Baby

After a scorching one-night stand with a sexy firefighter, I realize I'm pregnant...with my brother's best friend's baby.

The Firefighter's Forbidden Fling

I knew a one night stand with my grumpy boss wasn't the best idea...but I didn't think it would lead to anything serious. I definitely didn't think it would lead to a surprise pregnancy with this sexy firefighter.

# GET A FREE COWBOY ROMANCE

Get Her Grumpy Cowboy for FREE:
https://www.MiaBrody.com/free-cowboy/

# LIKE THIS STORY?

If you enjoyed this story, please post a review about it. Share what you liked or didn't like. It may not seem like much, but reviews are so important for indie authors like me who don't have the backing of a big publishing house.

Of course, you can also share your thoughts with me via email if you'd prefer to reach out that way. My email address is mia @ miabrody.com (remove the spaces). I love hearing from my readers!

# ABOUT THE AUTHOR

Mia Brody writes steamy stories about alpha men who fall in love with big, beautiful women. She loves happy endings and every couple she writes will get one!

When she's not writing, Mia is searching for the perfect slice of cheesecake and reading books by her favorite instalove authors.

Keep in touch when you sign up for her newsletter: https://www.MiaBrody.com/news. It's the fastest way to hear about her new releases so you never miss one!